Falling for BENTLEY

Shawnté Borris

This is a work of fiction. Names, places, characters, media, incidents, and brands, are either the product of the author's imagination or are used fictitiously. The author acknowledges the trademarked status and trademark owners of various products referenced in this work of fiction, which have been used without permission. The publication/use of these trademarks is not authorized, associated with, or sponsored by the trademark owners.

Copyright © 2014 by Shawnté Borris
Editing by Raelene Green of word·play by 77peaches –
A division of 77peaches enterprises, LLC
Cover Designer © by Wicked by Design
Formatting and interior design by JT Formatting
Cover Photographer: Made in 81 Photography – Shawnté Borris
Cover Models: Ashley Verbeek & Dalas Venning
Beta & Proofreading: On The Same Page Beta & Proofreading
Onthesamepage.proofing@gmail.com

All rights reserved. Without limiting the rights under copyright reserved above, no part of this publication may be reproduced, stored in or introduced into a retrieval system, or transmitted, in any form, or by any means (photocopying, recording, electronic, mechanical, or otherwise) without the prior written permission of the above copyright owner of this book.

First Edition: March 2014
Library of Congress Cataloging-in-Publication Data

Borris, Shawnté
   Falling for Bentley/Shawnté Borris – 1st ed
      ISBN-13: 978-1495277511
      ISBN-10: 1495277518

   1. Falling for Bentley—Fiction. 2.Fiction—Romance 3.Fiction—Contemporary Romance

http://shawnteborrisauthor.com/index.php/en-ca/

Other Titles by Shawnte

With Love

The Game, Kirsten Backhard (Book One)

Falling for Bentley (Part One)

The Game, Derek Backhard (Book Two) 2014

Catching Haley (Part Two) 2014

This book is solely dedicated to the one and only Lacy Almon.

breathe ... no tears

I cannot for the life of me thank you enough. You have been my biggest supporter from the very beginning, enough that you became my assistant and best friend. The hours that you put in I can never repay you.
Your words of encouragement, stories that you share or phrases that put me in my place not only follow me in my writing but also in my daily life.

Not only have you and your family taken me in but also my family, and now both children refer to you as Auntie Lacy with the funny accent. From the very bottom of my heart, I love you and thank you. This book is yours! XOXO

Readers: What you don't know, is this book is a surprise for Lacy, she knows nothing about what's inside. What Lacy also doesn't know is that she had the final say on many of the details. Yes, I did lie to her on many occasions, but I figured it was okay considering I am an author, and I do get paid to tell great stories. ☺

Shawnté: *What was your first date with Chris like?*
Lacy: *Haha it's a funny story, just a sec...*

Our first supposed to be first date has been a big debate throughout our marriage. He tells everyone that I stood him up, but I didn't. LOL
Our first official date we went to Pizza Hut, I know exciting! He bought me flowers and candy; I still have the flower petals. We had pizza, warm beer, and the jukebox was stuck on a Hank Williams Jr's song. We laughed a lot, and to this day his sense of humor is still amazing. Chris has always had a lot of self-confidence, so much that he told me I broke his heart when I stood him up so it made him more determined to take me out. After our dinner date he drove me back to my tiny apartment and the look on his face was priceless when I told him he couldn't come in. He told me I was going to be a challenge for him but he would figure me out. (My hubby was known for being a player before I met him, lol) It's hard to describe that date; it was just funny. The food and beer was awful and that damn music. That pizza hut is still there and we still go back, but now we bring our son Avery.

Prologue
Haley

I TRUDGED UP the stairs to my apartment with sore feet, carrying the last box from my classroom and a heavy briefcase full of final papers that need to be graded before the end of the school year.

"Whoa, Haley, let me grab the box for you."

"Hey, Jerad, I didn't see you there." I passed the box to him before digging into my purse for my apartment keys. "Thanks."

"No problem. What are neighbors for? My mom taught me right, you know. When I see a pretty damsel in distress, I can't help but offer my services," Jerad said with a smirk.

"Remind me to thank your mother next time she's in town," I teased.

Jerad grabbed his chest in a mocking manner, "Always, the thanks goes to my mother."

I opened my door wide enough to let Jerad in with the box. "Just put it on the kitchen table." I tossed my briefcase and purse on the couch and slowly slid off my shoes, letting out a moan as I sank into the welcoming cushions.

"Why do you wear those shoes if they hurt so much?" he asked as he sat beside me on the couch, pulling my feet into his lap and rubbing them.

"Mmmm, that's feels great." I laid my head back on the armrest of the couch.

"Seriously, Haley, I don't get it. Sure the shoes look good, but they can't be all that comfortable."

It was my turn to look horrified. "Do not sit there and insult my shoes. They've done nothing to hurt you! Why are you being so vicious to them?" I teased.

Jerad laughed, "Okay." He put up his hands in surrender. "I'm sorry. Can I make it up to them and take you to dinner tonight?"

I slowly took my feet out of his hands and sat up, "Jerad…"

"Look, I get it. You don't see us like that, but, Haley, I like you. I think you're funny and sexy as hell. I'm not asking for a relationship, or to marry me. All I'm asking for is dinner."

I shifted uncomfortably in my seat, "Thank you for the offer, Jerad, really, but I am swamped with work. This last week of school is the most hectic for me."

"How about we order in then?"

"Persistent, aren't we?" I teased, kind of.

"Is there a boyfriend, or something, I'm not aware of?"

"No boyfriend or play toys such as yourself." I nudged his shoulder, "But I do think it's time I get to work grading papers," I said in a polite voice.

Jerad got up and walked to the door, "My offer still

stands, when you're ready, call me and I'll give you a night out you will never forget."

I shut the door and rested my forehead against it, sighing. I looked over to my shoes and gave them a dirty look. I hated wearing them, but I teach in a privileged school, with uppity parents, so it's expected of me to look the part.

I grabbed them off the floor, walked into my bedroom, and tossed them into the closet. I undressed in front of the full length mirror and looked at my body. Sure, I've lost the extra weight I carried in high school, but I still see the chubby girl waiting to be accepted, and I could still hear them calling me *thunder thighs*. I threw on a pair of yoga pants and my favorite rock band t-shirt before heading into the kitchen to make some dinner.

Waiting for my grandmother's chicken pie to heat in the oven, I pulled out the last of the essays that needed grading. As the timer on the stove went off, I threw the papers off to the side, frustrated. "Did any of these kids read the damn book?" I complained to myself.

After I finished eating, I packed my lunch, placed it in the fridge and finished up the dishes. I dried my hands and walked back into the living room. I'd just sat down on the couch when my phone rang. I checked the caller ID as I pulled it out of my purse, just to make sure it wasn't Jerad. I smiled when I saw it was my papa.

"Hi, Papa." I gushed.

"Hi, Haley, I hope I'm not calling too late," he snickered.

"No, you're fine," I said rolling my eyes. Just because I live three hours north from him he thinks there is a time change. "I still have a few papers to finish grading before tomorrow."

"Are you ready to be home for the summer?"

"I am. This has been the longest ten months ever. Why I ever accepted to teach junior high this year is beyond me."

"That bad?" he asked concerned.

"Oh, Papa, if you only knew."

"Grams wants to know when your last day of school is."

"The students finish on the twenty-fifth, but I'm not done 'til the twenty-eighth."

"When do you plan on leaving for the ranch?" Papa asked.

"As soon as possible; I can't wait. This city life is driving me absolutely insane."

"Are you sure you don't mind running the ranch while Grams and I do some traveling?"

"Heavens no. I think I can manage weeding the garden, watering the flowers and pounding a few staples into the fence," I laughed.

"We are quite sure you can. We just wanted to make sure we aren't taking you away from anything."

"Papa, is this your way of asking if I'm bringing a male companion home?"

"No," he said quickly, "It was your grandmother asking."

"Sure it was," I teased.

"It was."

"Papa, I'll see you and Grams in two weeks."

"We love you."

"I love you both more."

I BELIEVE, AT one point or another, my mother loved my father, but I think with him traveling all the time for his job, she just got tired of dealing with life all on her own. One night when my dad came home, my mom decided she was going to have a girl's night out. But my mom's night out was a little different than most moms'—it's been twenty-four years and she still hasn't come back.

My dad tried to find her over the years; he even came close a few times, but my mother always managed to get away. Finally accepting defeat, my dad quit trying. My father hired a nanny so I was able to travel with him until school started, then he sent me to the best private schools money could offer. Once high school came, my dad and I had a long talk about how alone I felt, and I wanted to be with my family. He said he couldn't quit his job, but maybe my grandparents were willing to let me stay with them.

The summer of my sophomore year, I moved to southern Arkansas and took up residency at my grandparent's cattle ranch. In my childhood years, I lived to spend every Easter, Thanksgiving, and Christmas at the ranch, along with my summers. My grams taught me how to behave like a lady and cook with the best of them. Papa taught me to work hard and to have a little fun. I got to stay in my dad's old room when he lived there. I didn't change a thing, and to this day I still stay in that room. Even now, as an adult, I can't wait to get back to the ranch.

"GOOD MORNING, MISS Wells."

"Morning, Mr. Krept." I stood from my desk and greeted my boss, the school dean.

"Please, have a seat, Miss Wells." He motioned me back to my chair as he took a seat in a desk at the front row.

"To what do I owe the pleasure of you stopping in?"

"Just seeing how your year went." he smiled.

"It was different. I enjoyed it, but I really think I want to go back teaching elementary school."

"I see you applied for the elementary posting."

"I did. Kindergarten and second grade are my favorite grades to teach, sir."

I started getting nervous and wiped my sweaty hands down my skirt.

"Miss Wells, the board has decided to hire a new teacher for that position."

"But I thought…Mr. Krept, when I took *this* position I was told I would be able to return to teaching elementary next year."

I noticed my boss shifting slightly in the seat, "Yes, you were, but things have changed."

"Why?"

He looked around my classroom before standing and walking to my desk. "Haley, your teaching is impeccable and we are fortunate to have you. This is why they chose what they did."

"Thank you," I gritted out.

"I hope you stay with us; however, if you choose not

to, I will personally write a letter of recommendation, as well as one from the school. I smiled at him, knowing once again, I got screwed over.

"Will you be attending the staff BBQ tomorrow night?"

"No, sir. I am heading home to the ranch. My grandparents are traveling this summer, and I told them I would tend to their ranch while they are away."

"Well then, I hope you have a terrific summer; keep in touch and let me know what you decided."

"I will, and thank you again, sir."

Bentley

"WHEN I SAY move. I fucking mean MOVE!" I yelled to the high school football team I help coach.

"Coach, come on. It's our last practice before summer, do we really need to be pushed this hard?" my little brother asked while hunched over his knees trying to breathe.

"Do you want to win the state championship this year?"

My brother, Travis, stood, "Of course."

I got in his face, "Then move!"

I admit, I ran the boys harder than necessary today, but damn it, I want my team to be strong. "All right, since your quarterback is being a whiney princess, everyone down and do one hundred burpees before you leave the field." Travis looked at me as if he was ready to pounce. I just rocked back on my heels and crossed my arms over my chest.

"Working the boys a little hard, aren't you, Bentley?" asked Coach Dudley.

"Maybe a little, coach, but I don't want them thinking just because my brother is the quarterback I'm going to be soft on them."

"Setting the pace?"

"Yes, sir." I acknowledged.

"Fair enough." Coach slapped my shoulder and walked away.

Once the boys finished twenty-five burpees I yelled, "All right boys, hit the showers. Once you're cleaned up, meet back in the gym. Coach Dudley wants to have a word with you."

"GOOD PRACTICE OUT there boys. I'm impressed with how football camp went this year. Once Coach Knight and myself review a few things, we will do call backs at the end of July so we can start practices in August. Don't be discouraged if you don't make the A or B teams 'cause all that can change quickly. I have a few house rules that need to be followed and there will be no exceptions, I don't care who you are. Do I make myself clear?" asked Coach.

"Yes, sir!" The gym echoed.

"First, all grades must be kept up; nothing under a C+. So if that means you need to get friendly with the nerds, then I'd suggest you start now. Second, anyone that is caught drinking will be instantly cut from the team. Third, everyone is expected to do twenty volunteer hours in the community throughout the year. Fourth, absolutely no hazing."

We heard a few groans and someone muttering, "What's the point of being on the football team?"

"Good question," I answered. "Being a part of a team is banding together as brothers. You are here to back each other, support each other. Work hard together, and play even harder together."

"If my house rules are too much for you, then by all means, leave now and don't let the door hit you in the ass on the way out," the Coach continued. "Last house rule. Don't get anyone pregnant. Is *that* clear?"

"Yes, Coach!" the boys roared in laughter.

"All right then, Thunderbirds on three," Coach chanted.

"Thunderbirds!" the team shouted.

"Oh, one last thing. As you all know, we are in need of new uniforms. I'm pleased to announce we have ourselves a donor that will cover all new uniforms, provided we help him on his ranch this summer. There is a sign-up sheet outside my office. I expect all of you to put your time in. Dismissed."

Travis and I walked out to the truck, "What was your problem today, Bentley?"

"No problem."

"You were acting like a jackass."

"Jackass or not, Travis, when I am on that field, I'm your coach. I will run practice as how I see fit. If you don't like it… then quit," I offered.

THE RIDE THROUGH town was quiet. I knew Travis was pissed off at me, and I felt bad, but I wanted to let him know he wasn't able to walk all over me. Travis is eight years younger than me. We are close, sometimes a little too close with the shit he can convince me to do. But I figured this is what big brothers are for. When I left high school to play college football our bond grew even stronger. My dad got hurt on the farm, so I stopped playing and came home. Since then, I showed Travis how to fix his truck, we'd go fishing every Saturday morning, and he would do my football drills with me every night to stay in shape.

"What is there left to be fixed out in the barn?" Travis asked, breaking the silence.

"Not much, I got most of it done this morning before practice. I just need help hanging a few gates in the maternity pen."

"Has Dad been out there to look at what we did so far?" my bother asked.

"No, but I imagine he was out there while we were gone."

"Think he'll have anything nice to say?"

"Not sure," I quietly replied.

"I wish he wasn't such a dick all the time."

"Travis." I warned.

"What? It's true, and you know it."

"He wasn't always this way, it's just since the accident. I'm sure it's tough on him, you know, not being able to help and do things on his own."

"That doesn't excuse him," my brother argued.

"I know," I replied quietly.

As we waited for the light to turn green, we both sat in silence, lost in our own thoughts.

"Bentley?"

"Yeah?"

"Do you ever want to just leave the farm?" Travis asked, still looking out the truck window.

"Why do you ask?"

"Just wondering, I guess." Travis shrugged his shoulders.

"I'd planned on playing professional football, then retiring to working on the farm."

"Do you miss playing?"

"I don't really think about it anymore."

"Why?"

"Dad got hurt, and the farm needs me." I said simply.

I pulled through the last street in town. "Do you want to stop by Maggie's and get a burger before we leave?"

"Not sure I can stomach a burger, man. You ran my ass pretty hard today."

I chuckled while I pulled into the parking lot. "You'll get use to it. What's the worst that can happen? Puke on the way home? It wouldn't be the first time."

"And not the last." Travis chuckled, as he hopped out of the truck.

"Hey, Maggie," we said when she greeted us with her welcoming smile.

"Well, if it isn't my two favorite football stars." Travis and I both leaned over the counter and kissed either side of her cheek. "Let me guess, two double cheese burgers, fries and cherry cokes?"

"You know it, Ms. Maggie," Travis smiled.

"Travis, why don't you go and grab a booth for you and your brother? Bentley, I need your help lifting a box in the kitchen."

"Yes, ma'am," we both replied.

"Bentley, why do these burgers always taste the best after practice, or on game nights?" Travis asked as he stuffed the last bite into his mouth.

"I don't know, brother, but I hope Maggie never stops flipping those burgers."

Maggie walk toward us carrying two more plates, "Thought you guys could use a piece of my homemade cherry pie."

"Maggie, I'm not sure if I have room for all this pie," Travis cried while rubbing his stomach.

"Nonsense. If your brother is going to be running his practices the same way he practiced, you'll need every carb I can get into your stomach."

"Hey," I complained.

Both Travis and Maggie laughed. And of course, we ate the pie.

"Did you sign up to help at the Wells Ranch?" I asked my brother, throwing some cash on the table.

"Yeah, since it will be quiet at the farm for the next few weeks, I signed up to help the first week."

"I hear Mr. Wells is a perfectionist."

"Really? Like I have no practice dealing with that, *Coach.*" Travis pushed my shoulder as he walked towards the truck.

"Smart ass," I replied.

Chapter One

Haley

THE SMELL OF the fresh air was all I needed to get my bearings back. How I missed the ranch and my grandparents. If only there was some way I was able to stay here and teach.

"Is that my sweet Haley I see walking to the house?" Grams gushed.

I ran to her in the garden and hugged her. "My goodness child, you are going to crush me."

"I'm sorry, Grams, I just missed you and Papa so much."

She held me at arms lengths, "Goodness child, when was the last time you ate?"

"Leave the poor child alone, Eleanor, she just got here."

"Hi, Papa."

"How was the drive?"

"Long, but good." I looked around the ranch, "It's

good to be home."

"I'm glad to see you still feel that way."

"Papa, this will always be my home, this is where my heart is."

"We definitely miss having you around here," Grams smiled.

"What are you doing in the garden, can I help?"

"Go to the shed and grab the fork and dig up some potatoes for dinner."

"Yes, Ma'am."

Papa walked me over to the shed and handed me the fork, "Are your bags in the back of the car?"

"Yes."

"I'll bring them up to your room."

"Papa, that's not necessary. I can bring them in after dinner."

"Nonsense. This may be your home, but until we leave tomorrow, you are our precious guest."

"Thanks, Papa."

"Mmm, Grams, this fried chicken is so good." My mouth was still watering as I took the last chicken leg from the plate.

"Knowing my baby girl was coming home how could I not make her favorite meal?" Grams replied, clearing the table.

I grabbed her wrist, "Grams, I got this, go finishing packing."

"Nonsense I'm an old lady, how many clothes do you except me to pack? With your Grandpa and I leaving tomorrow you need to go over everything he has planned for the ranch. Now go on out to the barn."

"Okay." I got up with my chicken leg and headed to the barn.

"Grams said you need to go over a few things with me?" I asked walking into the barn.

"The list is on the table in the corner," Gramps said, not looking at me while cleaning the horse stalls.

- *Paint barn and sheds*
- *Weed garden and flower beds*
- *Cut the grass*
- *Cut down the back forty*
- *Move the east cows over to the west*
- *Fence the back half of the quarter*
- *Build a pull shed for the quad and garden tractor*
- *Clean out and tidy the calf barn*
- *Haley, have some fun!*

"Uh, Papa, this is a pretty heavy list for me to do on my own." I uttered, overwhelmed.

Gramps laughed, "Silly girl, I know you won't be able to do all of that. I just need you to oversee everything."

I looked up at him, "I don't understand?"

"I made a deal with Coach Dudley."

"The high school football coach?" I questioned.

"Yes. I said if his team would help you out for the two weeks I'm gone, I will sponsor their new jerseys."

"Papa, that's a lot of money."

"It is sweetheart, but the ranch needs some TLC and I'm getting too old. I thought it was a fair trade."

"Why wouldn't you wait 'til you're back?" I asked,

puzzled.

"Because I know you can handle it, and I know you won't let me or Grams down."

"I won't," I said. "When are they expected to be here?"

"Tomorrow afternoon. I think starting off at the fence will be a wise choice."

"Okay."

After helping Papa move things about, we went back into the house and had a cup of tea before turning in for the night.

"I'm glad you're home," Papa said, patting my head before he went up for bed.

"Night, Papa."

Grams came around the corner, "Would you care for another cup, sweetheart?"

"No thanks, Grams. I'm pretty tired, I think I'm gonna head to bed, too. I'd like to go for a quick run before you and papa leave tomorrow."

She took my cup and placed her palm on my cheek, "I'm so happy you are here. Things around here are just too quiet when you are gone."

"I love you, Grams." I replied, leaning into her hand.

Bentley

ONE EYE BARELY open, I glanced around the room, desperate for it to stop spinning. There's a faint moan beside me, and when I carefully turned my head towards it, I saw brunette hair splayed across the pillow and down the back of a naked chick. My eyes slowly skimmed down to the small of her back—my favorite part of a woman's body.

I stopped when I recognized the Celtic tattoo and quickly lifted the sheet to see if I had my briefs on, I did. I slowly sat up to look for any evidence of last night's shit show. No condom…no wrapper, thank God. Lube and a vibrator? What the hell? I don't remember using either of those things.

"What are you doing?" giggled Mandie as her cold claws rubbed my back. I tried to straighten out of her grip. "Baby, relax, let's finish what we started last night," she whispered in my ear before kissing the side of my neck.

"Did we?"

"No, you passed out before the party really got started. I had to use my vibrator to finish the job before I could finally go to sleep."

"Uh, sorry about that." I lifted her hands off me.

"Why don't you make it up to me, Bentley? Like the good old days back in high school. I miss this," she growled, grabbing my dick.

I shot out of the bed and scrambled for my pants.

"Where are you going?" Mandie grabbed my shirt and threw it over herself.

"I…ah…I need to go," I stuttered, trying to put my shoes on without falling flat on my face.

"Bentley," Mandie whined.

Bang-Bang-Bang, "Bentley, get your ass up. We gotta go," Curtis yelled.

"Thank Christ," I mumbled under my breath as I put

on the other shoe.

"That's it? You're really going to leave me like this, wet and wanting you? Needing you to fill me?" moaned Mandie.

"Sorry, Mandie, but I gotta go. Curtis and I already made plans." I opened the door and looked at my best friend.

"Bentley, before you walk out that door, you better think long and hard. There may not be a third time."

"There shouldn't have been a second," I toss over my shoulder and ducked just in time to miss a glass as it shattered on the wall in front of me. I closed the door and looked over to Curtis, laughing his ass off. "Let's get the fuck out of here."

I looked in the back seat of Curtis's truck and saw his gym bag. Zipping it open I was lucky enough to find a t-shirt. I smelled it before I put it on, "Smells clean enough." He started the truck and put down the windows.

"Looks like it's gonna be another hot one today." I said leaning out of the truck window letting the breeze take some of my hangover away.

"Seriously, dude?" probed Curtis.

"I know."

"She's like a walking dick rash, not to mention your ex-high school squeeze and my girlfriend's sister. Thank God the crazy stopped at Mandie," he continued.

I groaned. "I don't remember much past the river."

"I knew you were drunk, but I didn't realize how drunk."

"Well, Curtis, if you were so sober, why didn't you stop me?"

"I tried, but you insisted that no one wanted a washed up farm hand."

I sat there for a few moments, "Sorry man."

"Don't apologize to me. It's not like my dick was going to turn green and fall off."

We pulled into Maggie's diner and grabbed a booth in the back.

"Morning guys. You're looking kinda rough there, Bentley," my brother's girlfriend said while passing us the breakfast menus.

"Hi, Whitney, Travis treating you good?" Curtis asked.

"Yes," she giggled. "What can I get y'all?"

"I think I'll start with a glass of Kool-aid and water please." I uttered, still looking at the menu.

"I'll have a coke and a glass of orange juice." Curtis replied.

"I'll be right back with those," Whitney smiled and headed towards the cooler.

"Dude that shit is going to curdle in your stomach." I groaned just thinking about it.

"Not everyone got as shit faced as you did last night. What the hell happened? I haven't seen you get that drunk in forever."

"I don't know, Curtis. My dad and I got into it again before I left."

"When are you going to tell him to fuck off?"

"I can't."

"Why? Obviously, you don't enjoy it anymore, but then again, neither would I having to work with your dad."

"I do it for my mom, the farm has been in her family for generations, and I'm sure she'd like to keep it that way.

Besides Travis is starting to throw hints that he wants to leave when he finishes high school. So it just leaves me."

"Have you considered talking to your parents about maybe buying them out or something?"

"No." I mumbled.

Curtis put down his menu and thanked Whitney as she set our drinks in front of us. "Maggie said don't bother looking at the menu. She already has your breakfast on the grill." Whitney grabbed our menus and headed over to the new customers that came in.

"Thanks, Maggie," Curtis and I both yell.

"Bentley, I don't get it, you hate the pressure your dad brings with the farm, you guys are always going head to head, and you haven't thought if you want to buy his ass out or better yet *leave*?"

"Something like that."

"Dude, that's fucked up," my best friend snorted.

"You don't understand, Curtis."

"I understand man, I do, but I'd start thinking long and hard on what you want. Don't you think it's time to start living again, instead of always being pissed off?"

"Bentley," Maggie spoke while placing my plate in front of me. "What Curtis is saying has some truth to it, and you know it." I looked up at Maggie. "Don't look at me like that, boy. You need to find what makes you happy, and not worry so much about the others. It'll bite you in the ass later."

"What's with all the tough love this morning?" I grumbled.

"I suggest you sit and have a talk with your mother, Bentley. You may even be surprised as to what she might even say." Maggie handed over Curtis's plate.

"Thanks, Maggie, it looks great, and smells even better." Curtis leaned over and smelled his food again.

"You're welcome, sugar."

Maggie patted my shoulder, "If you ever come into my diner smelling like a keg again, I will plunk your ass into my dishwasher. Do I make myself clear?"

"Yes, ma'am," I sulked.

"Good, now you boys enjoy your breakfast, and say hi to your mamas for me."

Curtis and I were just finishing up breakfast when the diner door chimed and in walked the most beautiful woman I have ever seen. My mouth must have opened a bit, because Curtis turned around to see what I was looking at.

"Who's that?" I whispered.

"Haley Wells."

"Who?" I asked again.

"Haley. We went to high school with her." Curtis shrugged and went back to eating his toast.

"I don't remember her."

"Sure you do. It's thunder thighs."

I looked at Curtis confused.

"Really, you don't remember her? You're the one that gave her the nickname." Curtis looked at me like I had lost my marbles.

I watched as Haley walked through the door and looked around the diner until she saw Maggie, and her face lit up like a damn Christmas tree. Maggie engulfed her in a huge hug and guided her towards the front counter and showed her a seat.

"What are you staring at, man?"

I shook my head, "Nothing."

"No you weren't. You were checking out thunder thighs."

"Stop calling her that."

Curtis turned back around to take another look at Haley, "She sure has shaped up nicely since high school."

"What is she doing now?" I asked still watching her.

Facing me, Curtis replied, "Do I look like the fucking high school reunion committee to you?"

"Don't be an ass. I was just asking."

Curtis drank the last of his orange juice. "Are you ready to go?"

"Yeah, man. I'll pay the bill and meet you in the truck."

"Good, I wasn't paying anyways." he laughed walking out to his truck.

Haley

I WOKE UP early to get a run in before seeing my grandparents off. I ran the five miles to town to grab some of Maggie's amazing cinnamon buns Grams loves so much.

Maggie and my dad used to date in high school, but when my dad chose to go away for college, Maggie decided to stay and help run her family diner, which she now owns. When I decided to live with my grandparents, she took me under her wing when things got rough and I needed a motherly hug. Maggie never did marry, nor have children of her own, but if she loved you, then you were one of her own.

I didn't let Maggie know when I was coming home for the summer; I wanted it to be a surprise. When I opened the diner door and looked around for her I was a little disappointed at first when I didn't see her. Then I saw her walking from one of the back booths. I couldn't help the smile on my face the moment I saw her.

"Haley!"

"Hi, Maggie." She engulfed me in a huge hug and guided me to the counter, insisting I have a seat.

"What a wonderful surprise. Why didn't you tell me you were coming so soon?"

"I wanted to surprise you," I said, sitting down on a stool.

"Best surprise of the summer, my dear." Maggie brought me over a glass of orange juice. "Now, what can I get you to eat?"

"No thanks, I'm good," I waved off.

"Darling, around here you do not get full on no thanks."

"I just stopped in to pick up some of your cinnamon buns for Grams before they leave this morning."

"Oh, I didn't realize that they were leaving so soon."

"They are," I smiled. "I'm glad they finally decided to take a well-deserved vacation."

"How many cinnamon buns, should I pack up?"

"Four please."

As I waited for Maggie to come back from the kitchen, I took a look around the diner and was happy nothing had really changed since I first moved here. It was just another place that felt like home, another reason I wanted to stay.

"I'd sure like to know what put that beautiful smile on your face."

I closed my eyes and cringed when I recognized his voice. I slowly turned toward him on my stool, "Bentley."

"What, I don't even get a hello?" he replied cockily.

"Why would I say hello to you?"

"Don't be that way, beautiful." Bentley gave me his mocking grin.

"What do I owe the pleasure of being in your presence?" I glared.

"Can't two good looking people sit together on such a warm sunny day?"

"Not when one of those people nicknamed me Thunder Thighs."

Bentley looked me up and down. "Looks like you grew out of that."

"Fuck off, Bentley, and stop wasting my time." I gritted through my teeth and mumbled, "Asshole," under my breath.

"I see you can still be snarky," he said as he played with the spoon on the counter.

I looked at his t-shirt then into his eyes, "At least I'm not a washed up football player still trying to relive his high school glory days." I turned back to the counter and took a sip of my orange juice, effectively ending the conversation.

Bentley tossed the spoon on the counter and left. "Seriously, what the hell did he expect?" I said loudly to myself.

"Who did expect what?" questioned Maggie with a container in her hand.

"Nothing, Maggie, everything is fine. I was just thinking out loud."

"Well, here are your treats," she handed me over the container, "Wish your grandparents a wonderful trip for me."

"Will do. What do I owe you?" I asked while digging in my sports bra.

"Girl, put away your money. You can repay me when you come over to visit one night."

"Sounds great, thanks, Maggie."

I was just about out of the door when Maggie asked, "How are you getting back?"

I looked down at my outfit, "Run, of course."

"Not with a box of my special over-the-top-cinnamon buns, you're not," she turned her head towards the half open kitchen door, "CJ, give Haley a ride to the Wells ranch, would ya?"

"It would be my pleasure, Ms. Maggie," replied CJ from the kitchen.

"That's not necessary," I said waving one hand.

"Child, do not talk back." She warned.

"Yes, Ma'am."

WAVING GOODBYE TO my grandparents was a little heartbreaking. As happy as I was they were finally taking a vacation after all these years, I still wanted to be here with them. I looked at my watch and decided to get a shower in before my workers showed up.

Throwing on a tank top with my jean shorts, I headed out to the shop to load up the quad trailers with the barbwire, staples, hammers, and extra gloves. Hearing the rumble of their trucks, I walked out of the shop to greet the boys.

"Hi, boys, welcome to the ranch," I smiled up at them.

"Afternoon is Mr. Wells around? Coach said that we would be working for him," a dark haired boy asked.

"My grandfather left on vacation this morning, so for the next two weeks you will be working alongside me." I replied in my teaching voice.

The seven boys looked at each other and smirked. The dark haired boy spoke again and lifted his hand to shake mine. "Great, my name is Travis Knight. This here is Bo, Andrew, Cody, Mack, JJ, and Cullen, but everyone calls him Twilight."

"Shut up," shoved Cullen.

"I can see why," I teased.

"It's a pleasure to meet you Ms...?" replied Cullen.

"Haley will be fine," I smiled. "I think today we will start on fencing the back quarter and replace any wire that looks weak or destroyed."

"Sounds good to us," all the boys replied.

"Great, then let's get to work." I turned and walked back to the shop. "Follow me."

Chapter Two

Bentley

I WALKED IN the house through the kitchen, and saw my mom pouring a cup of coffee. "Morning, Mom." I walked over and kissed her cheek.

"Hi, sweetheart, would you care for a cup of coffee?"

"Please." I leaned over my mom and reached for my favorite Garfield coffee cup.

"I see some things never change," my mom laughed.

"Yeah," I replied quietly.

Mom sat at the kitchen table and watched me pour my coffee. "Bentley?"

"Yeah, Mom?" I asked, turning around.

"Come sit." She padded the seat beside her, "Let's talk."

I pulled out the chair and sat across from my mom. I looked into her eyes and noticed how tired they were. "Mom, are you feeling okay? You look tired."

"That's what I wanted to talk to you about." She held

onto her cup with both hands.

"Where's dad?" I asked looking towards the living room.

"He's not here, I asked Uncle Chris to take him fishing today."

I let out a small breath of relief.

"Bentley, I need to talk to you about the farm." I looked up at my mom, and she had a grim expression on her face. "I know you are not happy here."

"Mom…"

"Sweetheart," she placed her hands on mine, "I know, and more importantly, I understand. Working with someone like your father since he got hurt can be …well, it can be a pain the ass." Mom and I both chuckled. Mom held my hands tighter, "I want you to know that I, no *we*, appreciate everything you do around here. You have become a very fine man, and I am very proud of you. We understand what you gave up for us, and it's something we can never repay you for, son."

"It was never a choice," I whispered looking down at the table.

"For you no, I don't think you gave yourself a choice. For us, Bentley…"

"Please stop…" I slipped my hands out from under hers and we sat quiet for a few moments.

"Bentley, I'm thinking of selling the farm."

"What?" I couldn't believe what I just heard.

"I wanted to hold out until Travis was old enough to make the decision to stay or go and even though he hasn't exactly said he is leaving, I'm pretty sure he's going to. Once he leaves you won't have help. I'm too tired looking after your dad, the house, and the farm books to even consider helping you out."

"What about hiring a farm hand?" I asked.

"We both know the farm doesn't have that kind of money, and trying to find someone worthwhile is even harder."

"What does Dad have to say about all this?"

"He's not happy of course, but then again, he never thought he'd be retired at the age of forty-seven either."

"Mom, we can work…"

She cut me off, "This farm has been in *my* family for generations, Bentley, so at the very end, it's ultimately my decision."

I swallowed, "What if I were to buy in, or we could sell off some land and cattle?"

"Those are options, too," Mom smiled. "But, son, you really need to decide what you want. Whatever it is, you will have *our* full support." Mom looked out the window and let out a sigh. "Bentley, you need to stay for the right reasons, *your* reasons. You need to be happy, and right now you're not happy. I can see it in your face every day, and as your mother, it kills me. You need to remember why you love it out here."

I wrapped my arms around her shoulders and kissed the top of her head. "I love you, Mom."

"I love you, sweetheart, more then you will ever know. No matter what decision you make, your dad and I will always love and support you."

I unwrapped my arms from her and went back to the table, "When do you want an answer by?"

"I was hoping by the end of August."

I almost dropped my cup, "That soon?"

"Yes, your father and I want things settled before the snow hits the ground."

"I see." I said, still in shock.

Mom turned so she could look me in the eyes, "I want you to leave, take a week off, and listen to your soul and see what it says. Now go pack a bag, and just remember to text me every once in a while to tell me you're alive."

"What about…"

"Uncle Chris said he'd help. There really isn't much to do this week, so we'll be fine."

"Are you sure?"

"Yes, go!" she smiled and pulled me into a big hug.

I headed up to my room, but stopped halfway up and leaned over the railing, "Mom?"

"Yeah?" she hollered from the kitchen.

"Does Maggie know what you're thinking of doing?" I asked.

"Yes. She's the one that helped me come to my decision."

My bags were packed, and I was nervous about where my thoughts were going to lead me. Do I want to leave the farm, or do I want to buy in? I lay in my bed, closed my eyes and just breathed. I must have fallen asleep, because when my phone went off, it startled the crap out of me.

"Hello?"

"Hi, Bentley. Coach Dudley here."

"Hey, Coach, what's up?"

"I was wondering if you could fill in for me at the Wells' ranch for a few days? I have an unexpected in-law situation, and my beautiful, determined wife insists we take them places while they are here to visit."

I laughed, "Coach, she's standing beside you, isn't she?"

"Yes."

"Tell Mrs. Dudley I'd love to take your place this week."

"Thanks, Bentley."

"Have fun," I teased while hanging up the phone.

I grabbed my keys off my dresser and my bag before heading out. I let Mom know I was leaving to go over to the Wells' ranch to give them a hand, and I'll most likely stay with Curtis

"I love you, Bentley."

Opening the door to my truck, I looked back at my mom and took a moment to see some of the stress was gone from her face, "Thank you, Mom."

SLOWLY PULLING UP to the ranch, I could hear the boys laughing. I got out of the truck and followed the sounds to the shop.

"So then, after his date left him in total disgust, he still stayed and watched the end of the movie," laughed Bo.

"Shut up, man. It's not like I knew vampires could make babies," Cullen complained.

"That, right there, is why we call him Twilight," taunted my brother.

Haley was bent over laughing, "Oh God, I wish I could have seen the look on her face."

"She was pissed. It was so worth watching the end of the movie just to see that," Travis roared.

"Wait…" she pointed to all of them, "you all went and saw the movie?"

"Well yeah, how else were we going to sabotage his date?" asked Mack.

"So you all stayed and watched the ending?" she asked, while holding her sides still laughing.

"We even went back and watched part two. Do you know how many hot chicks went to see that movie?" asked JJ, giving Bo a fist pump.

Haley shook her head, "You guys are funny."

"Come on, Haley, I'm sure you did stuff like that in high school?" asked Travis.

"Can't say I did. I moved here the beginning of my sophomore year, and by that time, everyone already had their groups of friends." Haley shrugged her shoulders.

She walked over to the workbench and bent down to grab something. I watched her as her legs stretched and her little bum pushed out and wiggled as she tried to untangle something.

"I think I need some help. Can someone lift the air compressor off this rope, please?"

My team was just standing there, mouths hanging open. I cleared my throat and walked in the rest of the way.

"Hi, Coach," the boys said in unison.

"Boys," I glared letting them know they been caught ogling her perfect ass.

Haley quickly turned around, losing her balance. Travis reached his arm forward just in time so she didn't fall. "Lucky bastard," one of them coughed.

"What are you doing here?" she asked wiping her hands on the bottom of her tank top.

"I'm the adult supervision," I replied.

"Haley, may I introduce my brother, Bentley, or Coach Knight," Travis offered.

Haley turned her head to my brother, "Coach Knight?" She took a step back and looked me over, "I know, Bentley. We went to high school together."

"No, shit," Travis snickered under his breath.

"Watch your mouth," I growled.

"Sorry, Coach," Travis backed away from Haley.

"I'm the defensive coach, actually. Coach Dudley is still the head coach," I offered.

Haley started walking out of the shop then she stopped turning to Bo, "Bo, would you mind getting that rope for me, please? I'm just going to run up to the house and grab the cooler I left on the back step."

"Yes, ma'am," he replied.

"Thank you," she muttered before practically running towards the house.

I hurried out, "Haley, wait." I grabbed her arm and she planted her feet glaring at my hold.

"What?"

"I just wanted to apologize for what happed at the diner this morning."

She gave me a funny look, "You're apologizing for being conceited at the diner, but you won't apologize for calling me names throughout high school and making my life hell? Nice, Bentley, real nice."

She spun back around, but this time stormed towards the house. I rested my hands on the back of my neck and wrung it. I let out my breath. Sometimes, I can be such an asshole. I went back to the barn, seeing my brother leaning against the door smiling.

Haley

I TRIED NOT to let him bother me. I thought I had put the past behind me. As I made it up the steps, one tear fell down my cheek. I quickly wiped it away; I will not let Bentley Knight get to me like he did in high school. No, I will not. This is my home, my territory, and I'll be damned if he takes that away from me.

Picking up the cooler, I headed back to the barn. "All right boys, are we ready to head out?" I asked throwing the cooler in the back of one of the wagons. "Since there are nine of us and only three quads, how do you boys want to do this?"

"Cullen and Bo are going to take one quad. Andrew, Cody and Mack are going to take Mack's truck out. Which leaves JJ, you, me and my brother for the other two." replied Travis.

Travis got down on one knee in front of me, with one hand on his chest and the other reaching for my hand, "Haley, will you do me the honorable privilege of riding a quad with me?"

"There will be none of that. Travis, get up." Bentley announced.

"I guess you heard the dragon," I nodded towards

Bentley. "I can ride myself." Walking over I patted the quad seat, "I think I can handle her."

"Fair enough," agreed Travis, snickering at his brother.

"Shut up and get on the damn quad, Travis," Bentley ordered.

I told the boys to go ahead and I'll follow behind shutting the gates as we go. I hopped on the quad and started it up. Putting on my work gloves, I saw Bentley walk up.

"Push back, Haley."

"Why?" I challenged.

"You are riding with me."

"No, I'm not," I replied snippy.

"Haley."

"Bentley."

"Haley, move back," he tried demanding again.

"No. If you want to get on, then you are riding with me. Hop on the back and don't touch me," I growled.

"Fine," he said as he threw one leg behind me to get on.

On the way to the back quarter I made sure I hit every damn hole, fast.

"Haley, slow down, it's not exactly comfy sitting on these bars."

I hit another big hole, laughing to myself, "What? I didn't hear you."

Bentley leaned down to my ear, "You are busting my balls."

I slowed down, "Sorry." I snickered.

"I'm sure you are," he ground out between gritted teeth.

I drove the rest of the way with a huge smile on my

face.

We finally got to the start of the fence line and the boys were lined up against Mack's truck, waiting for my directions.

"Okay, boys, let's do this." I clapped my gloves together, "I'll start the first wire and Cody can string out the line. The rest of you can staple as we go. We are doing a four wire fence, but with all of us, we should get a good portion of it done today, and whoever comes out tomorrow will finish it."

The boys were a great help, they took out everything we needed and set it up. I was just about ready to start the wire when Bentley tried pushing me out of the way.

"What are you doing?" I demanded, holding on tight to the fence stretcher, as Bentley tried to take it out from my hands.

"Starting the fence."

"I know. I'm doing it." I tugged back.

"Look, I can get it tighter than you. Just give me the fence stretcher," Bentley instructed.

"Fence stretcher what?" I challenged, holding it still between us.

"Haley, *please* give my pig-headed brother the fence stretcher," called out Travis.

"I'd be delighted to Travis," I replied in my kindest voice, shoving the stretcher into Bentley's chest before walking away. Grabbing a hammer and a pail of nails I walked my way down the fence line.

"DAMN, IT'S SO hot out today," Bo said, taking off his wife-beater and wiping the sweat off his forehead.

"I know, man. I'm surprised we aren't melting," replied Cullen.

"Twilight, vampire's don't melt, they sparkle in the sun," teased Bo, trying to take off Cullen's t-shirt, "Come on, Cullen let's see you sparkle."

Cullen shoved him back, "Fuck off, Bo."

The boys started laughing, cheering Bo on.

"All right, boys, let's stop and see what's in the cooler," I offered. "Since everyone is picking on Cullen, he can sit with me and pick the first drink out of the cooler."

"Thanks, Haley," muttered Cullen.

"No worries, Twilight," I laughed.

Rolling his eyes, Cullen dug in the cooler, "Is this Mrs. Wells' sweet tea?"

"It is," I winked.

"Awesome," he said, excitedly opening the lid and downing half of it.

"Any more in the cooler?" asked JJ, "I love her sweet tea. She makes the best in church."

"Nope, I just saw the one bottle in the fridge," I shrugged, downing a bottle of water.

An hour later, I was done, so I told the boys it was a wrap for the day. "Thanks, guys, for all your help. I can't believe how much we got done today."

"I'd say another two hours tomorrow and we should be done, Haley," Andrew announced looking down the fence line.

"I think so, Andrew." I smiled at the boys. "If you are coming tomorrow, let's start at eight so we can finish early.

I hear tomorrow is supposed to be hotter. When the fence gets done, why don't you boys bring your swim trunks and cool off in the pond afterwards," I offered. "Then, if y'all want to stick around, we can BBQ in the afternoon."

Everyone else said they were coming back, except Cody. "Sorry, Haley, but I promised my mom I'd help her in the garden tomorrow."

"No worries. I'm just glad you were able to help today."

"I can come on Thursday," he offered.

"Sure, come whenever you can make it. I don't want to be taking any of you away from your family, or other commitments you have already made." I said, securing the cooler to the truck and looking over to the boys.

"The team will be here, we made a commitment," Bentley announced roughly.

"All righty then." I saluted before hopping up on the tailgate of the truck. "Bentley, will you be the last one out and close the gates, please?"

Back at the barn I told the boys to leave everything in the barn and to not bother putting it away, since we'll just be using it tomorrow. After I sent them on their way, I walked into the house and slouched in a kitchen chair. I forgot how exhausting it was working in the sun, but I can't say I'm sore, since the boys pretty much pushed me out of the way and did everything themselves.

I took another look at Papa's list, deciding tomorrow the boys can finish the fence while I cut the grass then weed the garden and flowerbeds. I made myself a quick sandwich before hopping in the shower and climbing into bed.

Chapter Three
Bentley

I DON'T UNDERSTAND why Haley got under my skin, but she did. Maybe it was her smell, or her smile, or how fucking great her legs looked in those sweet-ass shorts. I gave my head a shake, trying to let go of the image of her, sitting on the tailgate, boobs bouncing, while I followed her on the quad.

Holding Curtis' fridge door open as I stared into space thinking of Haley, I once again found myself wondering what she was doing at this very moment. Maybe she was soaking in the new claw tub Curtis installed for her grandmother.

"What are you doing?"

I jumped, hitting my head on the freezer door, "Fuck!"

"Serves you right for holding my fridge door open for the last five minutes."

Rubbing the top of my head, "Hey, man, what are you doing home so soon?" I turned and shut the fridge door.

"Whoa, dude! Put the tent away." Curtis cringed while covering his eyes.

I immediately covered my crotch by reopening the fridge door. "Beer?"

"Yeah."

I passed him the beer before closing the door, hoping that my dick had time to deflate. "I thought you were going to Loran's tonight?"

"I was, but she has PMS or something, and was totally bitchy, so I came back home." We walked over to the living room and settled in to watch *Sports Center*. "If I didn't love her so much...sometimes I just wish I could say, 'Put the crazy back in the box.'"

I laughed, "Well, you should have known crazy runs in that family. Seriously, look at her sister, Mandie."

Curtis was quiet for a moment before he blurted out, "I want to marry her!"

I spit out my beer, "What?"

Curtis got up and set his beer on the table. "Bentley, I'm going to ask Loran to marry me."

"Seriously?" I asked stunned.

"Yeah, man. I love her."

"It's only been six months," I coughed.

"I know, but shit man, I fell in love with her before she even decided to go out with me."

I stood and gave Curtis a bro hug, "Congratulations, man. I'm happy for you."

"Thanks, man."

Curtis grabbed his phone and walked into his bedroom while I went back to the couch. I must have fallen asleep because when Curtis opened his bedroom door it woke me.

He had his jacket and boots on.

"Where are you going?" I asked sitting up.

"To Loran's."

"Going to grovel?" I teased.

Grabbing his keys off the table, he smirked, "Already did that, now it's time to make up."

I shook my head while Curtis shut the front door on his way out.

I rubbed my hands over my face then looked at my watch, eleven o'clock. My phone rang while I was brushing my teeth. I tried to catch it, but I didn't make it in time. Noticing it was Travis; I called my brother back right away.

"Hey, brother what's up?"

"Are you by yourself?" Travis asked quietly.

"Yeah, why?"

"Bentley, I did something really dumb tonight."

"What?" I asked unsurprised.

"I had sex with Whitney."

I sat on my bed, "Okay."

"Bentley, you don't understand, I forgot to wrap up."

"Oh."

"Yeah."

I took a deep breath, thinking about what I was going to say to my brother.

"Bentley, what am I going to do?"

"Don't panic. Is she on the pill?"

"She says she is."

"Do you believe her?" I asked seriously.

"I do."

"Then my guess is you're probably okay."

"Really?"

"Yeah, man." I heard my brother let out a breath. "Did you and Whitney talk about it afterwards?"

"Yeah, she said she was okay with what happened and that she wasn't worried because she has been on the pill for a while now."

"My advice, just remember to always wear a condom, Travis."

"Yeah, yeah."

We were both quiet for a minute, "Travis?"

"Yeah."

"If she gets pregnant, we'll figure it out together," I reassured him.

"Thanks."

"That's why I'm here. See you tomorrow at Haley's."

"Night."

I put my phone on the nightstand and lay in bed, watching the ceiling fan turn. I couldn't believe it, my best bud is getting married and my brother is having sex. What's next? Getting Haley to fall in love with me? Even that thought made me laugh out loud. Turning over, I set my alarm for five am so I could get a good work out in before heading to the ranch.

GRABBING MY TWO water bottles, I headed down to the football field to start my work out. I was on my last chin up on the goal post when I noticed someone running on the track. I jumped to the ground, grabbing one of the water bottles, and walked over to see whom it was.

As I drew closer, I noticed it was a woman. I'm usually doing drills this time of morning, and I've never seen anyone out here unless they were cutting grass. She was working on her last corner facing away from me when I walked onto the track. I watched as she gave it all she could, and this chick had some power. I should send my boys over and get her to teach the team a few things.

I watched as her blonde hair swayed with every step, her body looked nice and lean, her ass was nice and tight and those thighs were strong enough to hold on to my waist. I kept watching as she rounded the last corner, now facing me. Her legs were long in her tiny running shorts, her stomach was small, but had a little give, just enough to get my hands on it without feeling her bones. Her boobs in the sports bra she was wearing looked magnificent. I couldn't help but let my mouth drop open. As my eyes went farther up to her face, the runner skidded and came to a full stop.

"Holy shit." It was Haley.

"Nice to see you, too, Bentley," she puffed, bending over to catch her breath.

"Sorry, I wasn't expecting you."

"Expecting someone else?"

"No." I couldn't say more; I just stood there and stared. As Haley stood up, I noticed little sweat beads all over her body and I wondered what her skin would taste like.

"Take a picture, Bentley. It will last longer."

I shook my head, "Huh?"

"I said, you may want to wipe the drool from your face," she laughed.

"Oh." I ran my hand across my chin before I reached out my water bottle, "Water?"

Haley took the bottle, "Thanks, mine is on the other side of the track."

Still unable to say anything else, I watched as she tipped her head back and poured a little on her chest before drinking. Watching her drink was the most sexual thing I have ever witnessed, not to mention all that water on her chest.

Handing over the now empty bottle, Haley said, "Thanks, I needed the cool down."

I took the empty bottle and smiled, "No problem."

"What are you doing here, anyways?"

I looked behind me to the football field, "I was just running some drills, to stay in shape. I can't really run a football team with a beer belly."

"I suppose not," she smiled.

"Well, I better finish the last mile I have left. Thanks for the water."

Before she could turn away I asked, "Can I run with you? I mean I still need to do my cool down run."

"Depends, are you going to trip me or something?"

"I wouldn't do that."

"Are you sure? 'Cause I think yesterday you would have."

I shifted uncomfortably, "Look, Haley, I owe you a big apology."

"For what?" she asked rubbing her hands together.

"I was a jerk to you in high school." Haley let out a flabbergasted snort. "Fine, I was a complete asshole, and I'm sorry."

Haley remained quiet for a few seconds, "It was years ago, Bentley. I'm over it, friends?"

I stuck out my hand, "Friends."

As she put her delicate hand in mine, I felt a tingle. I looked into her eyes, and I knew she felt it too when she instantly stepped away.

"Ah, I better go, Bentley. I want to grab a few things for the boys before they get to the farm."

I didn't even have a chance to say anything before Haley was off running to the other side of the track.

Haley

OH MY GOD, did I just flirt with Bentley? I did. I couldn't run fast enough to the other side of the track. Once I opened my bag and pulled on my tank top, I looked over to see Bentley still watching me as I headed to the parking lot.

Shit, what am I thinking? This man was so mean to me in high school. Every day it was something with him, or his posse. The more they teased me, the more weight I put on. It took me years to get over the feelings that were left behind. What pisses me off the most is he sees me today and acts as if none of it mattered. God, I hate him.

I was so mad as I drove home I forgot to stop at the store and grab the few things I needed for the BBQ. I looked in Grams' cupboards to see what she had, chips and homemade cookies, that'll work. I went to the freezer and pulled out some hamburger to whip up some patties then I tossed a batch of dough in the bread maker before stepping outside to feed the dog on the porch. I could hear the trucks before I could see them. I snickered, "Boys." I walked down the driveway to greet them.

"Hey, boys," I waved.

"Hi, Haley," I got back in unison, while they stayed in the trucks.

"I was thinking that y'all could finish the fence while I work the flowerbeds and weed Grams' garden."

"Sounds good to us," JJ smiled.

Travis leaned over the seat and slapped JJ's shoulder, "Stop looking at her like that."

"What? She's hot."

I blushed.

"Well, you are."

"Thank you, JJ. Now you boys get to work and I'll meet you at the pond this afternoon."

"Great," said Cullen.

As the boys slowly drove towards the barn I yelled out, "Could someone please grab some lawn chairs from the shop and throw them in Mack's truck for the pond?" Cullen waved so I knew he heard me.

I decided to start in the garden and dig out a few potatoes to make a potato salad. I was bending over, picking peas, when I heard a loud cough behind me. I jumped and my butt went straight into someone's crotch. Then strong arms wrapped around my waist to keep me from falling forward into the dirt.

"You okay?" he whispered in my ear.

"Bentley?" I said, turning in his arms to face him. "You scared me."

"Really? The dog has been barking since I drove up the driveway."

I looked over to Buddy, sprawled out in the grass napping. I looked up at Bentley with a raised eyebrow and stepped out of his arms.

We stood there in an awkward silence, "Well, I should probably head in and start lunch, I'm sure the boys will be hungry when they finish. Will you be joining us?" I asked while grabbing my pail of vegetables. Bentley was looking everywhere but at me.

I slowly started walking around him when he grabbed my wrist. I looked up to his eyes and saw sadness. Instantly, I wanted to reach my arms around him and tell him everything was going to be fine.

"I'm sorry, Haley. I'm so sorry for the way I treated you in high school."

"You hurt me."

"I know," he whispered.

"You left me with scars that took years to overcome." I could feel my eyes tearing up.

"I'm sorry."

"Answer me one question, Bentley." The look in his eye quickly changed to determination. "You must answer it truthfully."

"I will."

I could feel the panic rise inside me, "Why?"

He took a deep breath before he answered, "I liked you. Hell, I still do."

I stood there, frozen, staring at him. Bentley started wringing the back of his neck with his hand.

I could feel a tingling sensation overcome me, the anger rising, before I slapped his face, hard. "You called me names and treated me like I was a piece of shit, Bentley. To the point where others followed what *you* did! Do you have any idea the damaged you caused? The years of therapy I went through to make myself believe I was worthy of someone, *of me*?"

Bentley stood there with this mouth hanging open. "That's right, Bentley, Mr. Football star. You made me feel like shit, and why? It wasn't like I did anything to you; if anything, I tried to stay clear of you." I was getting angrier with every word that spewed out of my mouth. "I couldn't date because of you. I'd rather be alone than have someone tear me to shreds all over again."

I couldn't hold back anymore, the tears came and the shaking began. Bentley took a step forward and wrapped his arms tight around me while I cried into his chest. I wasn't sure how much time passed before I could feel Bentley rubbing my head whispering, "I'm sorry, so, so sorry. Please forgive me, Haley. Please let me make this up to you." He must have repeated this ten times before I snapped out of it and out of his embrace. I cleared away my tears and eyed Bentley as he swept one last tear away.

"I'm so sorry, beautiful. I'll do anything to take away the hurt and pain I caused."

"Thank you," I half smiled.

"Friends?" he asked hopeful.

I took in a calming breath, "I may be able to try, but I won't be able to forget."

"I'm hoping to replace those memories with good ones of us *together*." He paused for a moment, "Friends?"

I smiled, "Friends."

I could tell Bentley was fighting the urge to hug me, so I grabbed my pail and said, "I better get going, lunch won't make itself."

"Thank you, Haley."

"Please don't make me regret this, Bentley. *Please*."

"I won't," he smiled. "I'm going to go check on the boys, what do you have them doing today?"

"Just finishing the fence today. It's pretty hot, so I told them when they were finished to go cool off in the pond and I'll bring out lunch."

"Do you need any help?"

"No, thank you," I smiled.

"Okay, see you later then." Bentley put his hands in his pockets and turned around.

"Wait."

He turned back around, "Yeah?"

"Could you please look at the calving barn door? It looks like it is hanging funny."

"Sure."

I DON'T KNOW why, but after my blow out with Bentley I felt better, lighter, and maybe a bit sexier walking back into the house. The phone rang just as I finished putting the potatoes on the stove to cook and slid in the homemade hamburger buns in the oven to finish browning.

"Wells' ranch, Haley speaking."

"Hey, bitch, whatcha doin'?" It was my crazy best friend, Carleigh.

"Making lunch for the boys," I smirked, always so forthcoming.

"Boys! What boys?" This time I let out a laugh, knowing she was now sitting up straight in her chair, clinging to the phone.

"Put your panting pussy away. These *boys* are still in high school."

"Well, you're no fun," she pouted.

"Papa said he'd sponsor their new football jerseys if they'd give me a hand around the farm while he and Grams are away."

"How many are we talking about?"

"Jerseys ...I don't know," I teased.

"Football players!"

"I have six today and seven when Cody is here."

Carleigh was quiet. "Does the football coach come out to help?"

"Umm, yes." I replied quietly—too quietly.

"Haley, what are you not telling me?"

"Their coach is Bentley," I whispered.

"What?"

"Bentley Knight, from high school, is their coach."

"The same prick that tormented you?"

I shifted uncomfortably, "Yes."

"I demand you get a different coach to help."

"You can't."

"And why not?"

"Carleigh, you live three hours away," I chuckled.

"I don't know what you find so funny. He was an asshole to you."

The timer went off on the stove, "Hold on a second I've got to pull the hamburger buns out of the oven."

"You did not make him Grams' fresh buns, did you?"

I took a seat at the kitchen table. "I kind of had to."

"Why?"

"I went for a run this morning on the high school track to get used to running on shale and gravel again, and I guess Bentley was there working out. Anyways, he came to see who was running. I guess no one is ever there that early besides the man that cuts the grass."

"Why are you drawing out the story? Just get to the good stuff already." poked Carleigh.

"Fine," I huffed. "I was running one of my last laps when I noticed Bentley on the track. I didn't know it was him; all I saw was tall, dark hair, and a chiseled chest. Carleigh, I could see the sweat beads glistening off his body."

Sssss sptsssss sssss

"What's the noise?" asked Carleigh.

"Shit! The potatoes are boiling over." I rushed over and moved the pot off the burner.

"I'm sure the potatoes aren't the only thing boiling over."

"Shut up," I laughed.

"Did you talk to him?"

"Yeah. He apologized for the way he acted in high school."

"Do you believe him?"

I sighed, "I think maybe I do."

"God, Haley, be careful. I'd hate for you to destroy the last five years you worked so hard to get."

"I will."

"Listen girl, I gotta go. I ordered pizza and the delivery guy should be here any second and I want to add more lip gloss."

"You're such a slut."

"I know." We both laughed as we hung up.

Chapter Four
Bentley

WALKING OUT TO the barn, I couldn't get the look in Haley's eyes out of my head as she'd slapped me. Granted, I totally deserved it, along with a swift kick to the balls. Thank God she didn't take it that far.

After fixing the barn door, I looked around and noticed someone must have started cleaning the stalls, but wasn't quite finished, so I found the wheelbarrow and finished sweeping them out. I laid new straw out in two stalls, just in case an emergency came up and Haley needed it.

Just as I finished with the calving barn, I could hear the boys coming up to the shop, so I decided to meet them there. I was just putting away some tools I found lying around when the boys came in laughing.

"Hey, Coach," said Andrew.

"Boys," I greeted them, "Fencing's done?"

"Yeah, it went quicker than we thought."

"Where's Travis?" I asked.

"He went up to the house to refill his water bottles," replied JJ, "It's getting pretty hot out there."

"I'm sure that's not the only thing he went for," coughed Mack.

I let out a growl.

"Sorry, Coach." Mack muttered.

"Don't disrespect women, especially the hands that feed you."

"Come on, Bentley, you have to admit that she's pretty hot," said JJ.

"Okay I'll give you boys that," I smiled, "But no more disrespectful talk, you got me? And that goes for anyone."

"Yes, Coach," the boys replied together.

After helping the boys unload the equipment I said, "Now that everything is put away, besides what Travis has on the quad, are you guys still thinking of heading to the pond?"

"I am," smiled Mack.

"I think y'all can head down there then. I'm just going to see what's taking Travis so long."

"We know," laughed the boys.

I just shook my head at them as I walked back to the house.

I could hear Haley laughing in the kitchen as I walked up the back porch steps, stopping just in front of the screen door, watching her laugh as her nose wrinkled.

"Hey, Bentley."

"What's up, Travis?" I asked, opening the door.

"Nothing, I was just telling Haley about the time I got stuck in the mud taking Whitney home."

"Thought you were pretty smooth taking her home on

the *back* roads," I laughed.

"What? I thought it was a good plan until I lost it and we had to walk a mile to the closest farmer to pull me out."

"What did she say?" asked Haley.

"What else? A woman's favorite words, *I told you so*."

Haley laughed again before turning to the fridge, grabbing some stuff.

"How was fencing?" I questioned my brother.

"Great, it went faster than we thought. We also did a quick sweep of all the fence lines and hammered in a few new nails and rewired two strings."

"Really? Thanks," Haley said from the fridge.

I casually tipped my head to the side to see if I could get a glimpse of her backside.

"It's amazing how fast it goes with five guys," replied Travis, poking my side, "compared to just me and you."

"You guys hungry?" asked Haley, carrying a big bowl to the table.

I stepped in front of her, "Let me get that for you." I took the bowl and placed it on the table.

"You bet, we're starving football players," Travis said, tapping his belly.

"I hope I made enough," Haley whispered, not sure of herself.

"I'm sure you did," I smiled at her.

"Bentley, did you hear the running coach quit yesterday?" asked my brother.

"No."

"Mom told me at breakfast."

"I wonder why." I asked no one in particular.

"Mom said she didn't know, but it's a small town, so

I'm sure we'll hear why in a few days."

"I wonder who'll coach then?" pondered Haley.

"Not sure," I answered honestly. "I'm sure they'll put an ad in the paper."

Haley handed Travis his two water bottles. "Here you go."

"Thanks."

"Travis, why don't you go put the quad away and grab the Gator for Haley."

"Sure."

"The keys are just there, hanging up. It's the one with the pig on it," Haley answered, pointing to a key rack by the door.

Travis grabbed the key on his way out the door.

"Are you just about ready?" I asked.

"I think so…oh crap." Haley ran to the door and yelled out, "Travis! Can you please grab the portable grill? I think it's in the white shed."

Shutting the screen door behind her she asked, "Can I get you something to drink before we head out?"

"Sure." I sat down at the kitchen table.

"Beer, or Coke?"

"I'm thinking Coke, since I'm here as Coach Knight, not Bentley."

Blushing, Haley passed me the soda, "Right."

TRAVIS AND I helped Haley load up the barbeque stuff on the gator.

"Are you guys sure I have enough food?"

Travis and I looked at one another and laughed,

"We're sure."

"Haley, you made enough potato salad to feed the whole team," I teased.

"Well, I don't want anyone to go hungry."

I placed the drink cooler in last and tapped the lid, "I think you're ready to go."

"Aren't you coming?" asked my brother.

I looked over at Haley. She was looking at the ground focusing on a rock by her sandal, knowing I had already given her the brush off.

"I didn't bring a suit or a towel. I wasn't planning on staying."

"Come on, Bentley. I know you always keep a gym bag in your truck so you have gym shorts."

"I can get you a towel," Haley said quietly.

Travis slapped me on my back, "Come on, brother, it's not like you have anywhere exciting to be."

"Alright."

Haley gave me small smile before going back in the house.

"You like her," Travis snorted.

"Shut up."

"Like, you really like her," he kept going.

I groaned.

"Dude, what's not to like?" my brother asked with a big grin.

I rolled my neck.

"Don't worry, I got your back, brother," Travis laughed as he walked to the side of the gator.

"I don't need you having my back, Travis."

"Yeah, you do. You suck when it comes to women."

"I do not. I can have my pick at any time, or place. In fact, I have," I stated.

"Ahem," Haley cleared her throat.

Travis and I whipped around in her direction.

"Shit," I said under my breath.

"You can say that again," Travis said back.

"Shall we go?" Haley questioned as she hopped in the passenger side of the gator.

"Travis, why don't you ride with Haley and I'll take my truck."

"I think that would be best. She looks kind of pissed," snickered my brother.

I glared at him hoping he got the message. *No shit.*

Getting to my truck, I dug under the passenger seat and grabbed out my gym bag and threw on my shorts. I turned over the key in the ignition as my phone started ringing.

"Hello?"

"Hi, Bentley, it's Whitney."

"Hey, how are you?"

"Good, I'm looking for Travis. Have you seen him?"

"He's at the Wells' ranch with me. Why, is everything all right?"

"Yes, he's just not answering his phone," she answered.

"I was just with him, and I didn't hear it ring."

"Oh," she sounded off.

"Whitney, why don't you come out and swim with us? Haley made enough food."

"Thanks, Bentley, but I'm working at the diner later today."

"Whitney?"

"Hmm?"

"Are you sure everything is alright?"

"Oh yeah, sorry I was just doing something," Whitney replied in a fake cheery voice.

"All right. I'll get my brother to call you."

"Great. Thanks Bentley." With that she hung up.

The drive to the pond was less than two miles. Just enough time for me to put my game face on, because *best friend* Bentley wanted to play.

Haley

"OH MY GOD, Haley, these are the best burgers ever," mumbled Bo through his third one.

"I can't believe it's your third one, you're going to puke if you try swimming."

"My mother starves me."

I slapped Bo's arm, "She does not."

"You're right, but damn these are good."

"They should be. It's Maggie's recipe," I said while picking at my food. I looked up and saw that everyone was staring at me, "What?"

"Maggie gave you the recipe?" Bentley asked astounded.

"Yeah," I uttered timidly.

"Well can I have it?" asked JJ.

"Sorry JJ, it's a family secret," I winked.

"Damn."

As the boys were finishing eating, I started putting away the food. I'd just dropped the ketchup into the cooler when Bentley's hand grabbed mine. "Come for a swim with me, Hales."

I looked up at Bentley, "You called me Hales."

"Is that not okay?" he asked, looking into my eyes.

"No one calls me Hales but my dad."

"Then I'll keep calling you Haley," Bentley smiled as he dropped my hand.

"No, it's okay. I like that you call me Hales, no one's ever called me that besides him." I grinned back.

"How about that swim?" he asked again.

I looked around at the guys, "Do you think it's appropriate? I mean, you are their coach and I'm well…whatever I am."

Bentley laughed, "Yes, Haley I'm sure. If we were in the city it probably wouldn't be appropriate, but our town has like a thousand people in it. It's pretty hard to not hang out together. Besides, most of these guys hang out at my mom's almost every weekend."

"Well if you're…" before I finished my sentence, I was hoisted over Bentley's shoulder screaming, "Bentley Knight, put me down!"

Bentley went running off the dock and jumped right in. I barely got a full breath in before my head went under the cold water. I came up spitting water out of my mouth.

"I'm going to get you for that!"

He had the nerve to wink at me, "I'm counting on it, *friend*," before he swam away.

"Cannon ball!" JJ hollered before soaking me again.

Bo tried to cannon ball, but it turned out to be more

like a belly flop.

"Oh, Bo, that has got to hurt," I laughed.

Bo laid flat on his back and rubbed his belly. "Maybe not as much if I'd stopped at burger two. I think I'm gonna puke."

"I told you. Just don't puke in the pond, the rest of us would like to keep enjoying our swim." I heckled as I splashed him before swimming over to Cullen.

"Hey, Cullen, what's up? You're pretty quiet today."

"Just thinking."

"Anything serious?"

"Nah," he said, sitting on the bank.

I went to sit beside him, "You sure?"

"I'm just trying to impress this girl and nothing works."

"What have you tried?" I asked as I wrung out my hair.

"Every pick up line you can imagine."

I cringed, "You did not just say that."

"What, what did I do wrong?" he asked, panicked.

I laughed, "Cullen, no girl likes a guy with cheesy pickup lines. We just turn around and make fun of you later for them."

"No, Haley, I have good ones, really," he insisted.

"Okay then, lay it on me," I snickered.

"Alright you asked for it." Cullen turned around to face me. "Haley, don't say things like that unless you plan to cowgirl up. I could give you way more than an eight second rodeo ride."

I burst out in full laughter, "You have *got* to be kidding me?"

"It's just the cowboy in me, Haley, get used to it."

I was holding on to my sides, "Stop, Cullen, stop, that's so bad."

"It is not," he argued.

"Oh, it is, Twilight," I said wiping away a tear.

"What has you in stitches?" asked Andrew as the rest of them swam over.

"Cullen. He just gave me the worst pick up line I have ever heard."

"Oh, I'm pretty sure I can beat him," said Andrew, "Ever since I heard your name and saw your ass in those daisy dukes you're so fond of wearing with those boots, I've been fantasizing about bending you over a bale of hay and taking us both to heaven."

"I've got one," Bo said next, "So...you think my tractor's sexy?" Now everyone laughed. "Shut up it worked... once."

Mack and JJ pipe up, "We have one."

"Bring it."

JJ cleared his throat, "Haley, I know you don't want to see guys unless they have a six pack, so I'm just going to work out so I don't have to walk around here sporting a keg someday." JJ and Mack bumped fists and yelled, "Boom!"

Rolling my eyes, I turned to Travis, "Alright, what's yours?"

JJ shoved Travis, "He's been going out with Whitney for so long, I doubt he remembers what a pick up line is."

"I do, too. In fact, I used one on her the other night," Travis said crossing his arms over his chest.

"Well then, let's hear it, baby brother," taunted Bentley.

"This is my kind of night, just you and me and the

back of my pickup truck."

Bentley looked shocked.

"Huh, that's pretty good, Travis. You boys should take a number from that." I stood up, "Well, boys, thanks for lunch and the swim, but I'm going to head in now."

"Do you need any help packing up?" asked Mack.

"No thanks. You guys did all the fencing, which would have taken me all summer. So stay and enjoy yourselves. Now that it has cooled down a little, I'm going to cut the grass. They are calling for rain tonight and possibly tomorrow."

"Should we come tomorrow if it is raining?" questioned Andrew.

"Not if it's raining, there's nothing you can do in the rain. I'll probably head into town and order some paint and stuff. I think the next thing we'll tackle is painting the barn and sheds. They are looking weathered."

"Sure," replied Andrew.

"Can you let Cody know, too?"

"You bet."

"Thanks for lunch, Haley. Really, it was great."

"Thanks, Andrew. You guys stay as long as you like, just bring the cooler back and drop it off on the porch before you leave."

Bentley stood, "I think I'm going to go, too."

"All right," I said before hopping into the Gator, "Later, boys," I waved.

After putting everything back in the kitchen and putting away the Gator, Bentley walked me back to the house. "Thanks for helping put everything away. You really didn't have to," I smiled.

"It was my pleasure."

"When is Coach Dudley due to arrive?"

"Trying to get rid of me so soon, Hales?"

"N-no, that's not what I meant," I stuttered.

"I know what you meant, I was teasing. Honestly I'm not sure. He is still entertaining his in-laws for a few more days."

I took a step up the stairs on the porch and turned towards Bentley, noticing how the wind was drying his hair curly. I just wanted to run my hands through it. It looked so soft.

"What are you staring at?" Bentley smirked.

"Me? Oh nothing." I shook my head.

"I bet you were wondering what the worst pickup line I ever used is."

"No, but now I am."

Stepping closer to me so we were almost nose to nose, he lifted a piece of my hair and tucked it in behind my ear and breathed, "Haley, sweetheart, just admit it, you want to ride me like a Harley on the country roads. It'll be so damn good, even John Deere will be jealous."

I just stood there gaping at him.

I heard Bentley chuckle, "That's what I thought."

He turned away and walked back to his truck. I grabbed the hand railing, still feeling his hand on me. I closed my eyes and when I reopened them he was standing in front of me. "Thanks for the towel."

I took the towel from his hands, "No problem."

Bentley smiled again before walking back to his truck, "See you tomorrow, Hales."

"Yeah, see ya," I quietly answered back.

Chapter Five
Bentley

AS I DROVE back to Curtis' house, the only thought on my mind was the feeling of Haley in my arms. God, I was so done for. "Ah," I turned up my radio and blasted some Eric Church.

After cutting his grass and weed whacking, I decided to hop in the shower to cool off. "Bentley, you home?" Curtis hollered out.

"Yep, I'll be out in a minute." Throwing on my sweats, I opened my bedroom door and walked into the living room and plunked myself on the couch.

"Thanks for cutting the grass, it looks good." said Curtis.

"It's the least I can do for letting me crash in your spare room."

"No worries." he replied while flipping the channels on the TV.

"How was your night after leaving here?"

"It was great," Curtis snickered with a huge grin.

"With that grin, I'm thinking I should be pretty proud of you."

"Yes, yes you should. I know I am," he proudly stated.

"That a boy," I patted his shoulder as I walked by.

"Anything exciting happen around here?"

"Beer?" I asked.

"Sure."

I handed Curtis his beer and popped my bottle cap. "Nah, I talked to my brother before I went to bed. Woke up, worked out, ran into Haley then helped at her grandparents ranch." I shrugged my shoulders.

"Where did you meet her at?"

"The running track."

"She's a runner?"

"She's got some good speed. I want to send some of my football guys over to her."

"Huh, I guess she would be with a body like that," my best friend offered up before taking a swig of his beer.

"Yeah," I mumbled, remembering her drinking my water.

"What's the plan for tonight?" inquired Curtis.

"I have to do some laundry and I was thinking of hitting up the grocery store."

"Cool. I'll come with you."

"What, no plans with Loran tonight?"

"Nah, I thought it'd be better if I let her get some sleep *tonight*."

"Looks like you could use some, too, with those bags under your eyes," I mocked.

Curtis stood up and slapped his chest a few times,

"This bull is good to go, *all* the time."

I went to my room to grab my t-shirt, wallet and keys. I walked past the bathroom, "Dude, are you pissing with the door open?"

"Looks like it, doesn't it."

"I don't need to hear you take a piss."

"I didn't realize I let my mother stay with me," chimed Curtis as he flushed the toilet and washed his hands.

While I was putting on my shoes I asked, "You do realize when you move in with Loran, you won't be able to do that, right?"

"Man, I'm going to *rule* the house. I'm even gonna make her hold it while I take a piss."

"You're an idiot," we both laughed as we walked out the door.

"Welcome to the Piggly Wiggly," said David, an autistic man the school usually has as their water boy during the football season.

"Hey, David," Curtis and I replied with smiles.

"Ready for the football season, Bentley?" David asked excitedly.

"You bet, buddy. Gonna be my water boy this year?"

"Yes, I am!" he shouted.

"Glad to hear it, man," I said placing my hand on his shoulder.

"Bentley, can I get a team jacket this year?"

"I don't see why not. Just get me your size, and I'll make sure you get one. Would you like a jersey, too?"

"Yes!" David yelled.

I laughed, "All right, catch you later, dude."

I was placing more fruits and vegetables into the cart

when Curtis came back with bags of chips, "What the hell, dude? The cart looks like a chick's."

"I need these things in my smoothies in the mornings."

"No, what you need is some pussy juice in your smoothies," Curtis ranted as he threw the chips into the cart. "I gotta go grab some bread and lunch meat."

"I'm going to go grab some milk."

Curtis hollered back to me, "Get some real milk, none of that skim milk shit."

I rounded the corner of the milk aisle and saw David talking to Haley.

"I'm David," he stuck out his hand.

"Hi David, my name is Haley," she delicately placed her hand in his.

"You are very pretty, Haley."

She laughed and placed her hand on her chest, "Thank you."

I grinned, thinking how nice she was being to him.

"David, I was wondering if you could help me?" Haley asked pleasantly.

"I can help with anything," David said excitedly.

"I'm making hot chocolate and I was wondering what is the best milk?"

"My mama always uses the pink lid milk," he said proudly.

"Two percent sounds good to me." She smiled while grabbing a half-gallon of the pink lid milk.

"You're welcome, and thank you for shopping at the Piggly Wiggly," David said before literally running the other way. Haley laughed as she watched him.

I pushed my cart beside her, "Fancy meeting you

here."

"Bentley, hey."

"What are you doing here?"

"Grams is out of some stuff to make hot chocolate and s'mores."

"Hot date?" I asked, more for my benefit to see if she was dating anyone.

"Nope, just the fireplace and a good book calling my name," she answered.

"So not dating anyone?"

"Bentley, are you fishing?"

"Me? No. I just might know of someone to set you up with, that's all."

She hugged her bag of marshmallows tighter, "I'm not interested, but thank you." Haley had a funny look in her eyes, I reached out for her arm, but she quickly sidestepped me and said, "I better be going. Have a good night, Bentley."

I looked at her, puzzled, "Night." Then it dawned on me what she said in the garden. *Great, another point in the shit pile.* I cursed myself.

Curtis dropped some more stuff into the cart, "Was that Haley?"

"Yeah."

"Are y'all friends now?"

"I think so."

"Cool."

"Ready to go?" I asked, pushing the cart down the aisle to the checkout counter. Stopping to get a few more things Curtis forgot, I managed to see Haley walk out of the store with David hot on her heels carrying her grocery bag.

"MAN, I HATE doing laundry, I wish clothes came disposable. Wear it and throw it out," Curtis complained while he folded his socks.

"It's not that bad."

"Dude, all your clothes fit in one load, and you were done like an hour ago. I've still got like four loads left."

"Shut up and fold," I heckled, throwing a t-shirt at him.

"Let's go grab some wings and beers at Pete's. I'm sure I can convince Loran to come over tomorrow and help me finish my laundry."

"Nah, man, I'm good. I was just thinking of putting a frozen pizza in the oven."

"Fine." Curtis mumbled having a bitch of a time folding his bed sheets, which eventually he just rolled them into a ball. "Whatever, so what's your plan for tomorrow?"

"I'm going to head over to the ranch tomorrow and give Haley a hand."

"I thought it's supposed to rain all day tomorrow."

"It is, but she has a few errands, and I'm going to tag along."

Curtis put down the jeans he was folding and looked at me, "Bentley, what are you doing?"

"What?"

"Dude someone like Haley, you don't play games with. I know we were assholes in high school, but I thought we out grew that."

"I'm not being an asshole. I seriously just want to be

her friend."

"Nothing more?" he questioned.

"Nothing," I replied, putting my hands up in surrender.

"Well, if you ask me…"

I interrupted him, "I'm not."

"If you ask me, you need to figure out your farm thing before you go chasing after Haley. If end up hurting her *again*, there won't be a friendship left to have."

Haley

I WAS STILL snuggled up on the couch with a fresh cup of coffee, listening to the drizzling rain and finishing one of my favorite books, when I heard a knock on the front door. Putting my cup down, I got up and moved to the door, wondering who would be here. I opened the door and was surprised to see Bentley.

"Bentley, what are you doing here?"

He lifted a bag from Maggie's, "Brought you some breakfast. May I come in? I'm getting a bit wet standing out here."

I quickly pushed the door fully open as Bentley grabbed the screen door, "I'm sorry. Please, come in."

"Nice pajamas."

"I like them," I mumbled as I looked down at my black tank top and my monkey pants. "Can I get you a cup of coffee?" I offered, walking into the kitchen.

"Please."

"How do you take it?" I asked, opening the cup cupboard.

"Just a bit of sugar."

I poured the coffee and was just about put in the sugar when I heard Bentley start reading out loud, "*And we were both completely and utterly...naked. My girl part was pressing against his thigh and my traitorous body wanted to rub itself against him. Oh my God...I'm a megahoe.*"

I dropped the spoon and went running into the living room to grab my book from his hands, "Bentley, give me that book!"

He held it above his head and kept reading, "*I lowered my head until our faces were inches apart, breathing the same breath and I drank him in. My eyes lowered to his lips and I didn't hesitate reintroducing them to mine. I kissed him, a soft closed mouth kiss, but deep nonetheless.*"

I jumped against his body, "Bentley, I mean it, give me back my book!"

Laughing, he bent towards my face, speaking softly, "*Breathing the same breath...*"

I stared at his lips, watching them twitch as he said each word.

"Your book..."

"Huh?" I asked, still looking at his lips.

"Here is your book," he slid it into my hand.

"Thanks," I whimpered, taking a step back. "What did you bring for breakfast?" I asked, desperately needing a change in topic.

Bentley lifted the bag off the coffee table, "Maggie's breakfast wraps."

"I-I'll just go grab us some plates and your coffee. I'll

be right back." Walking back into the kitchen, I noticed butterflies in my tummy.

Licking some of the ketchup from my fingers I asked, "You never really answered my question."

"What's that?" Bentley replied, licking his bottom lip.

"What are you doing here, it's raining. I told everyone not to come today."

"I thought I'd run errands with you today," he answered as he picked up his coffee cup and took a sip.

"Why?"

"Because I said I would yesterday."

"When?" I asked surprised.

"When I was giving you back the towel I borrowed."

"Oh," I muttered, feeling my cheeks turning warm.

I DAMPENED MY hair and put some mousse in it to make it somewhat bouncy and curly. I added some mascara and lip-gloss and I was pretty much ready to go. I went to my closet and grabbed a pair of dark wash skinny jeans, a t-shirt, and my favorite sweatshirt before heading back downstairs to the living room where I last left Bentley.

"You ready to go?" I bounced off the last step.

Bentley turned the TV off and stood up, staring at me. "You look great."

"Thanks. I'll just grab my rubber boots from the back door then we can go."

"Do you need me to grab your purse or something?" asked Bentley.

"Nah I'm good. I never carry a purse; those things are a pain in the ass. I just put my debit card and some cash in my back pocket and chap stick in this pocket," I answered, as I tapped my front jean pocket.

Bentley opened his passenger door for me and offered me the seat belt. "I'd offer to put it around you, but that's a little out of the friend code."

"We wouldn't want that." I took the seat belt from him and clicked it into place as Bentley shut the truck door and walked around the hood to his side. The smell in Bentley's truck was yummy, coconut maybe, and very clean.

"Where to?" Bentley asked while hopping in.

"I need to go to the hardware store and see if they have any barn paint."

"Red, I'm assuming," he said, putting on his own seat belt.

"Yes, but do you think the guys would mind if I got white as well so they could paint the trim? I don't like how everything is either all red or all white."

"Is white trim what you want?"

"Yes."

"Then white trim is what you'll get, Hales," Bentley smiled as we drove away from the house.

"So, Bentley, tell me about yourself. Like what you did after high school?" As soon as I asked the question, I noticed his hands clenching the steering wheel. "You don't have to tell me if you don't want to," I said in a small voice.

He let out a breath before answering, "No, it's okay. This is what friends do, right? They talk to each other, let each other know stuff, right?" He took a deep breath and began, "I got a football scholarship to the University of Texas in Austin."

"Longhorn."

"All the way, baby," Bentley beamed. "I was accepted as a general defensive player, but I more or less played middle linebacker."

"Rough spot to be in," I cringed.

"Sometimes."

"Did you get hurt often?"

"A separated shoulder once, and my knee makes a funny popping sound sometimes."

"What did you take in college?" I probed, shifting towards him.

"I went for my bachelor of science in agricultural studies."

"Wow."

"Haley, you sound impressed, like a dumb jock can't get an education," he teased.

"Those are your words, not mine, Bentley," he gave me a pained look. "That's just a demanding course load. It must have been hard while playing football."

"It was at times, but it paid off in the end."

"And then what?"

"Well, I was almost drafted into the NFL…"

"What happened?" I wanted to sit closer to him, knowing there was an interesting story waiting.

"Nothing. My dad got hurt, and I had to come home and help them on our farm."

"Oh." I went to reach out my hand, but pulled it back. "How did he get hurt?"

"Long story short, one of the grain truck hoists was

stuck in the upright position and wouldn't come down, so my dad climbed on top to see what the problem was and slipped. His back hit the ground pretty hard, and he was knocked out for a bit. He still doesn't remember exactly what happened."

"Is he alright now?"

"Yes and no. He can't really do any heavy lifting anymore, or bend too much without excruciating pain."

"That must be so frustrating."

"You don't know the half of it, Haley." He breathed deeply.

The rest of the trip to town was quiet, both of us lost in our own thoughts. I was happy when Bentley finally turned on the radio. A Miranda Lambert song started to play and before I knew it, I was bouncing my knee to the beat and started singing along. Bentley sang with me on each chorus while I smiled as I looked out the window smiling.

We pulled up to the hardware store and Bentley put the truck in park. "I'll get your door for you." I took my seat belt off and readjusted my sweatshirt before hopping out of the truck with Bentley's assistance.

"Why thank you, kind sir, I'm much obliged."

"You're welcome, pretty lady," he mocked back with a twang.

He went to grab my hand, but I stopped him.

"I just wanted to say I'm sorry. It's not easy talking about my dad and my *almost* career."

I turned to face him, "Why would you say that?"

"Come on, Haley, everyone knows I am just a washed up farm hand."

I placed my hands on his chest, "Bentley, I don't think

that, and I'm sure no one that really matters does, either."

Chapter Six

Bentley

SEEING THE SINCERITY in her eyes almost made the words feel true, like none of it mattered. I placed my hands on top of hers, leaned in closer and quietly said, "Thank you."

"Well, if it isn't my two favorite students." I looked up and saw my eleventh grade science teacher, Mrs. Harris, stopping on the sidewalk in front of us. Haley turned around, but I noticed she didn't step away from me as she said hi.

"Haley, I heard you were in town for the summer."

"I am," Haley said proudly.

"Did I also hear you are teaching at Lawrence Academy?"

"Yes Ma'am. I've been there for four years."

I could feel Haley slouch a little, so I placed my hand in hers and ran tiny circles on the top of her hand with my thumb, giving her support.

"It's a pretty impressive school to be teaching at for your age. How do you like it?"

"I love it." I felt Haley take in a deep breath; apparently, I wasn't the only one with secrets. "What are you doing now, Mrs. Harris?"

"I am the new principal at the elementary school now."

"How wonderful, my favorite grade to teach is second."

"What do you teach now?" asked Mrs. Harris.

"My first two years, I taught second, then kindergarten, and last year was my first year teaching seventh grade English."

"How was that?"

"A hormonal train wreck." Both ladies laughed.

"So is high school." Mrs. Harris laughed.

"Are you going back in the fall or are you staying around here?" Good thing I was standing close, I really wanted to know the answer.

Haley let go of my hand and started fiddling with the sleeves of her sweatshirt.

"When they asked me to teach junior high last year, I was told I could go back to teaching elementary school this coming year. But on the last day of school, the dean came and told me they hired a new teacher for the position and they wanted me to continue teaching junior high."

I could hear a little tremble in her voice, and I knew Mrs. Harris did, too, when she placed her hand on Haley's arm. "Well, Haley, you must be one great teacher if that is the case. Any school would be lucky to have you."

"Thank you."

"Well, I must go before it starts raining again. It was

great seeing you both. Haley, when you have a chance, stop in and visit me."

"You still live on Linsey Street in the yellow house?" Haley asked.

"I do."

"Then I guess I'll see you later, Mrs. Harris," Haley said as she walked away.

Haley took a few steps away from me, but I reached out and grabbed her hand again, "Haley?" She turned around and faced me, "Do you want to talk about it?"

"Not much to say," she half smiles. "I'm going back to the city, which I hate living in; to a school where they care more about what I wear than actually relating something to my students; and I have a neighbor that is constantly hassling me to go out with him."

I instantly felt angry and jealous. "Has he hurt you?" I gritted out.

"No, no nothing like that." Haley shook her head before changing the subject. "I'm going into the hardware store, coming?"

"In a minute."

"Find me in there, okay?" she smiled at me.

"I'll be there in a minute, promise."

I watched her walk away as I flexed my hands a few times and took a few deep breaths to calm myself. I sat back in the truck to think. Here I am, in the same situation as Haley. Lost in what we want, backing down from the fight of what we need and what makes us happy. Maybe Haley did understand what I'm feeling; maybe she truly believes I'm not a washed up farm hand.

WALKING INTO THE hardware store, I saw Henry talking to Haley about paint.

"Would it be possible to have the paint delivered when it comes in?" asked Haley.

"We can do that for you."

"Great, let's do that then." Haley smiled.

"Should we put that on the farm account along everything else that you need?"

"That would be great, Henry, thanks."

I walked up behind Haley. "Hi, Bentley, I'll be with you in a minute. I'm just going to finish up with Haley." Henry gestured.

"No, thanks, Henry, I'm actually here with Haley today," I smiled.

"Then let's go up to the front and put the order together." Henry and I waited until Haley went first. I loved watching her ass in those jeans. I heard Henry clear this throat. I looked at him and shrugged my shoulders, *what*? Henry chuckled until we reached the counter.

"Look over everything and make sure it's right then sign at the bottom. I'll call you when it's here. Shouldn't be more than two days." Henry said, sliding the paper over to Haley.

My phone rang in my pocket. Taking it out, I saw that it was the farm calling. I put my hand on Haley's shoulder, "Haley, I'll meet you outside, I just need to take this call."

"Okay," she looked up and smiled. Her smile is cute, and I love her mini dimple that comes out. I shook my head while heading outside.

"Hello?"

"Hi, Bentley, it's Mom."

"Hey, Mom, what's up?"

"Just checking in."

"I'm good. How are you and Dad?"

"Oh, we're good, sweetheart. What are you doing today?"

"I'm in town with Haley. She had a few errands to run and I thought I'd help her."

"Haley who? I don't recall you being friends with a Haley." Mom probed.

"Haley Wells. She's the granddaughter of Eleanor and Wyatt. The football team is helping out at the Wells' ranch in exchange for new uniforms."

"The same ranch Travis is helping out at this week?"

"That's the one, Mom."

"Travis and the boys say she's quite pretty."

"Have they now?" I tried hard not to sound irritated, but I don't think I succeeded.

I could hear the humor in my mom's voice, "Yes, and Maggie says she is absolutely delightful."

"Mom, you called to talk about Haley, not to check in," I laughed.

"You caught me," she laughed back.

I pulled the phone away from my ear and took a breath. "Mom, I see Haley coming out of the hardware store, so I've got to go. I'll catch you later."

"Oh, just wait a sec, hon, your dad wants to talk to you."

"Sure."

I smiled at Haley as she approached me, she mouthed, "Everything okay?"

I nodded my head yes, before I answered my dad. "Hey, Dad."

"Since you are in town, do you mind stopping in at John Deere and picking up that seal, they called this morning and said it came in."

"I can do that."

"I see you later then."

"Bye, Dad."

I hung up the phone and slid it into my pocket, "Would you mind if we took a detour to the John Deere dealership? I need to pick a seal up for my dad."

"Sure but it's gonna cost ya."

I moved closer to her, "It will, will it?"

"Yep, I see a strawberry milkshake in my future," she mocked.

"Oh, I think I can handle that," I said while opening the passenger door for her.

I HELD THE door open to the dealership for Haley as she walked and said, "It's going to be awhile, look at all the farmers here." I put my hand on the small of her back, hoping she wasn't going to flinch away, "It rained, so they have down time. It's a good day to grab parts and stuff." I walked us over to the line at the parts counter.

Standing in line for twenty minutes, I realized my wallet was in the glove compartment of my truck. "Hales, I'll be right back, I forgot my wallet in the truck."

"Sure, take your time," she answered back, looking at the gloves in the display case.

I lightly touched her arm, "You okay here alone?"

Haley looked around the dealership, "I think I'll be okay, I don't see any boogie men in here, unless one is hiding behind those pails of oil."

"Smart ass," I grinned before I left.

Walking back in, I saw Haley's shoulders shaking, like she's trying not to laugh out loud. I walked up beside her and whispered in her ear, "Hey, what's so funny?"

She turned and faced me with tears in her eyes. "Just wait, you'll see."

Not even ten seconds later, an older lady with a red coat was pouncing around the store yelling, "What is taking so damn long?" Haley leaned in towards me, still trying not to laugh as the woman continued, "Jesus Christ, it's not like we're ordering parts, we're just picking up a fucking knife for the combine," she ranted in front of her husband.

"Oh," I said. Haley just nodded her head, still holding on to me.

The lady took another walk around the store and stopped in front of her husband again and screeched, "Fucking hell!" before she stormed out. By this time, Haley was leaning fully into my side with her head pressed tight into my shoulder laughing. I wrapped my arm around her and enjoyed the feeling.

Backing away from me, and drying her tears she said, "That was the best freaking moment of the day."

I smiled at her, "Yeah, it was." already missing her touch.

"Here's your part, Bentley, sorry it took so long," Cole said, smiling over at Haley.

"Cole, have you met Haley?"

He runs his hands down his shirt, "No, I don't believe I

have."

I rolled my eyes at him, "Haley, this is Cole, his dad owns the dealership." Cole held out his hand, and it took everything I had in me to not smack it away so he wouldn't touch her.

"It's nice to meet you, Cole, but if you'll please excuse us, Bentley is taking me to lunch," Haley replied sweetly, shaking his hand.

I just about whipped my head over to her, but I managed to keep my eyes glued to Cole to watch his response. He withdrew his hand slowly and smiled back, "Enjoy your lunch."

"We will, and thank you." Haley grabbed my hand and turned us towards the door. I looked back at Cole and grinned.

Haley

"BURGER AND FRIES?" I asked Bentley.

Bentley stopped us just before we got to his truck, "What was that?"

I scrunched my forehead not understanding, "What was what?"

"The whole grabbing my hand and telling Cole were going for lunch."

"You're not hungry?" I asked testing the water.

"Hales."

"Fine, he gave me a creepy feeling. I'm sorry I used

you."

Bentley stood taller and smirked. "Bentley, knock it off." I slapped his chest.

He walked around me to open my door again, "You can use me any time you want, Hales," and he winked at me. "Want to go to Maggie's or somewhere else?"

"Maggie's please, she makes the best milkshakes."

Driving over to Maggie's, I thought about how easy going my day has been so far with Bentley. Sure there were intense moments, but all in all, it's easy to hang out with him. And I liked the fact he tried to claim ownership of me with Cole; that guy is just creepy, and he needs to brush his teeth a little more than once a week. I shivered with the thought of his hand touching mine. I must remember to wash my hand as soon as we get to Maggie's.

"Are you cold? I can turn on the heat," Bentley asked concerned.

I rubbed my arms and shook the thought of Cole being interested from my head, "No, I'm good."

"Okay." But out of the corner of my eye, I saw Bentley turn the heat up a little which made me grin inside.

Walking into the diner, I turned towards the bathroom, "I'm just going to wash the Cole germs off my hands, why don't you grab a booth and I'll meet you there."

"It's okay, I'll wait here for you." I quickly walked to the bathroom, wondering if Bentley saw this as a date?

"Do you care where we sit?" Bentley asked me as I returned from the bathroom.

"Maybe a window, the sun is starting to come out," I replied, eyeing a booth in the middle of the diner.

"Sounds good to me." Bentley looked at the waitress

and waved.

"Hey, Bentley, just help yourselves to a seat, I'll be right with you," said the waitress. She was beautiful, my height, brown hair with the prettiest green eyes I've ever seen, but definitely younger than me.

"Thanks, Whitney."

I slid into the booth facing the back of the diner while Bentley slid in across from me. "Still want that strawberry milkshake?" Bentley asked.

"Yes, please," I answered and grabbed a menu.

"Sorry about that." I looked up and saw the waitress smiling at Bentley. I don't know why but I kind of wanted to claw her eyes out. I let out a little laugh at the thought.

"Whitney, have you met Haley Wells yet? Her grandfather owns the ranch Travis and the football team are working at."

"No, I don't think I have." Whitney bounced on her heels facing me and stuck out her hand. "Hi I'm Whitney, Travis's girlfriend."

Just like that, I had a smile on my face as I shook her hand, "It's nice to meet you. I've heard wonderful things about you. Travis really cares for you."

"Well he better, because I love him to death. Now what can I get you two to drink?"

"Two strawberry milkshakes please," Bentley ordered.

"Coming up."

"Is Maggie in?" I asked looking towards the kitchen.

"I'm sorry she's not in 'til four."

"I just wanted to say hi."

"I can tell her for you, if you'd like," Whitney offered.

"It's okay, maybe I'll stop in later," I smiled.

"I'll be right back with your milkshakes."

"So tell me, how do you know Maggie?" Bentley asked while stretching out his body and getting more comfortable in the booth.

"Well, she and my dad dated in high school and then my dad decided to go to college somewhere else, and Maggie wanted to stay here. When I moved in with my grandparents, Maggie became like a second mom."

"Does your dad come here often; I don't recall ever meeting him?"

"He comes once, maybe twice a year, his job keeps him pretty busy on the road."

"What does he do?"

"He helps design machines for big rig companies, kind of like an engineer."

"Are you two close?"

"We are," I answered happily. "I talk to my dad at least once a week, if not twice."

"What about your mom?"

"What's with all the questions, Bentley?"

"Nothing, I'm just trying to get to know my new friend. If you don't want to answer the question, you don't have to."

"With my dad traveling all the time for his job, my mom just got tired of dealing with life all on her own. So she decided to split and leave me with my dad; neither one of us has seen or heard from her since."

"That's rough," Bentley said, laying his arm across the back of the booth pulling his t-shirt taught across his chest.

"It's okay. Well, I don't mean okay she left her child behind, because seriously, who does that, right? But everything worked out; I travelled lots with my dad and when I couldn't any more he sent me to one of the best schools in the country. Then, in high school, I asked to live with my grandparents, and well, you know the rest," I shrugged.

Whitney walked over and handed us our milkshakes. "Have y'all decided what to order yet?"

"I think I'll get the pork chops with the hash brown casserole and a side garden salad with a vinaigrette dressing, please," I said then put my menu back in the holder.

"I'll have a steak sandwich, medium with a loaded bake potato and steamed vegetables, Whitney."

"Good choices, it shouldn't take too long."

Looking straight at me, Bentley replied, "We're not in a hurry."

Whitney looked down at the two of us and smiled before she walked away to put in our order.

I waited for Bentley to take a sip of his milkshake before I asked, "Well, what do you think?"

"You're right, they are good. I can't believe I haven't had once since I was a kid."

"Do you want to know Maggie's secret?" I asked leaning in towards the table.

Bentley met me half way, "Yes."

I looked around the diner before I crooked my finger, telling Bentley to come closer, "She not only uses real strawberries, but she adds a bit of jam, too."

"Don't worry, I'll take that info to the grave," he whispered back.

I leaned closer to the milkshake, "Nah, don't worry about it. My grams makes them the same way. Who do you think taught her how to make them?" I took a big drink, but kept my eyes on Bentley.

I pulled back a little, and Bentley swiped my bottom lip with his thumb then stuck it into his mouth. "You had a little milkshake on your lip, thought I'd get it for you."

"Thanks," I sighed back.

"Did you always like it here? I mean with your grandparents and all," he asked.

"I love it here, always have. I couldn't wait to spend my summers here as a kid. Then, when I was old enough for school, I counted down the days until Thanksgiving, Christmas, spring break, and everything else in between to get back here."

"If you had the opportunity to stay here, would you?" Bentley asked with a different tone in his voice I didn't quite understand.

"I'd need a job to stay," I replied truthfully.

"If you had that, would you stay, even after all the bullshit I put you through?"

I didn't even hesitate, "Bentley, I would give anything to stay here."

"Even giving up your job at the academy? Schools here can't pay you what you make there."

"True, but if I could teach and live here, I would. Money isn't everything, Bentley."

Bentley sat back and looked like he was thinking about what I said. I drank my milkshake while I waited for him to process whatever he was going after. "Hales."

"Yeah?" I said looking up to him.

"I really am sorry for what I did and said to you in high school."

I placed my hand on his, "I know, and I accept your

apology. I don't think you are the same person any more. If you were, I wouldn't be sitting here."

RUBBING MY BELLY and pushing my plate away, I announced, "I'm full. That was so good. I can't believe I forgot how great the cooking is here."

Bentley laughed, "I can't believe you ate it all. I don't even know where you put it."

"My ass."

"Well if that is where it went, I'm grateful, because girl, your ass is de-lish-ous."

"Funny. Does that line work often?"

Bentley smirked, "I don't know, does it?"

Rolling my eyes, I couldn't help but giggle.

"Want to share a piece of strawberry shortcake?"

Chapter Seven
Bentley

JUST AS I asked Haley if she wanted dessert, I saw Mandie walk into the diner. I hope to hell she doesn't see me. It's not like I could hide behind a menu, or anything. Like that wouldn't look weird.

"Hey, you okay? You zoned out on me." I heard Haley say.

"Yeah I just…" *and fuck!*

Mandie stood beside Haley, looking her up and down with evil eyes. I could tell what was going to happen before Mandie even opened her mouth. I tried to stop it, but Haley beat me to it, "May we help you?"

Mandie let out a sneer before walking over to me and running one of her troll nails down my cheek, "You can't, but Bentley here sure can."

"Mandie, get your hands off me." I shifted in the booth to get some space between us.

"Bentley, don't be like that, you know what we had

four nights ago was magic. When you are done here with—whatever this is—why don't you stop by my place and we can finish where we left off. And you can get the t-shirt you left behind." she purred.

How in the fuck did I ever find this bitch attractive?

"Jesus, Mandie, would you leave Bentley alone?" called out Whitney.

"What? I wasn't doing anything wrong. I was just saying hello to Bentley, and politely introducing myself to his friend."

"Oh, cut the shit," Whitney huffed. "Haley, this is my second cousin, Mandie. Please don't mind her, she was just leaving."

"I am not." Mandie snarled, "I was just going to join them."

"Well, don't bother. I was just about to bring them their check," Whitney hissed.

"Nonsense, I'll just slide in beside Bentley, and we'll have dessert. What is Ms. Maggie's pie special today?"

Haley stood, "You know, I just don't feel like having dessert. Whitney, it was wonderful to meet you. Anytime Travis is at the farm, please don't hesitate to stop in, okay?" Then she turned to me, "Bentley, I'll meet you outside, whenever you're ready."

I watched as Haley placed the napkin on the table before walking out of the door. I slid out of the booth and got in Mandie's face, "I don't know what the fuck kind of game you're playing, but knock it the hell off." Mandie stood there, her mouth hanging open, as I continued, "I can't believe how you just acted, were you always such a conniving bitch?"

"You used to think it was my best quality," she growled back.

"Yeah, in high school. When are you going to grow the fuck up?" I dug in my pocket and shoved some cash in Whitney's hand on my way to the door. I looked back at Mandie, shaking my head, "What the fuck was I thinking, *ever* going out with you?" Then I hurried out of the diner, hoping to save the rest of the day with Haley.

"That's fine!" Mandie yelled just as I reached the door. "I was done with you anyways. I need a real man that is actually going to make something of himself, someone other than a washed up nobody." I stopped, but decided to not make a scene. I pushed the door open and stepped outside.

I walked over to where Haley was sitting on a bench just a little down the street. "Haley, I'm so…"

Haley stood and cut me off, "Don't apologize for what she just did. You and I both know nothing would, or could, control that mouth of hers."

"Was she always like this? For the life of me, I can't see what I ever saw in her." I said more to myself. The look in Haley's eyes gave me my answer.

"That was then, and this is now. The difference between the two of you, Bentley, is you grew up, and she stayed in high school."

I pulled her in for a hug, "You, Haley Wells, have one of the biggest hearts I have ever known."

Dropping Haley off at her ranch was just something I wasn't ready for. I knew she still had a few things to do in town, but after the whole Mandie disaster, Haley just wanted to go back to her place.

"Thank you for letting me tag along today," I said trying to lift the mood in the truck.

"Thanks for the ride and for lunch. I guess I should pay you back, since I pretty much left you in the diner with no option except to pay." she spoke as she reached for her back pocket.

"Haley, put your money away, I don't want it," I almost growled.

She shifted her hand away from her back pocket, "Okay, well, thanks again."

I walked her to the door, prolonging the goodbye as long as I could. I felt like such a dick for what happened at the diner, and I have a feeling any leeway I had with Hales, just went back to square one. I leaned on the porch railing while she opened the front door, "Thank you, again, Haley, for hanging out with me today."

She turned around and smiled, "I enjoyed myself, well, minus the unpleasant visitor."

"Could we maybe do it again sometime?" I gripped the rail, trying to hide my nervousness.

Haley moved in front of me, "Why, Bentley Knight, are you asking me out on a date?"

I pulled my hand off the rail and took a step closer, lacing my fingers through her hair, "Hales, will you please see me again tomorrow?"

"I'd like that," she answered shyly.

I leaned in and placed a small kiss to her cheek, "Tomorrow."

I waited in my truck until she went inside before I pulled away.

On the way back to town I decided to call my brother to see if he wanted to meet up.

"Hey bro, what you up to?" Travis answered the phone.

"Just calling to see if you want to hang out, maybe go for a run and do some weights at the gym."

"Needing to talk?" my brother asked in a serious tone.

"Yeah."

"Cool. Come pick me up at the farm. Want me to grab your gym shoes?"

"Please. See you in ten."

I hung up the phone, knowing Travis and I needed to have the conversation about what he and I really wanted out of the farm.

A mile into our run on the treadmill, Travis looked over to me, "Bentley, are you going to leave the farm?"

"I don't know."

"What do you want?"

"I don't know," I answered back.

"Do you miss playing football?"

"I don't know."

"You don't know, or you don't want to be honest with yourself?"

I ran for a bit before answering him, "I'm scared. What if what I want doesn't make anyone else happy?"

"Who cares about anyone else, Bentley, you need to only think about you."

"I don't want to let Mom down."

"You're not going to let her down. Mom is giving you the out, if you want it, man. She's not going to turn you away, or love you less, for whatever decision you make."

"Yeah and what about Dad? He's been on that farm, growing it into something. I'm not fond of the idea of throwing that away on him," I answered back.

"Bentley, I hate to sound like an ass or an ungrateful son, but when Dad got hurt it kind of left him without an option. It's no different than someone having a heart attack and having to leave his job early. Dad was just handed an early retirement."

"When did you get so smart, little brother?" I questioned.

"When my big brother became my best friend," Travis answered simply.

I smiled over to him, "First one to hit five miles picks the weight training routine."

TRAVIS AND I left the gym all sweaty, "Dude, you stink," he said, pushing me away from him.

"It's not like you smell any better, little douche bag," I taunted, shoving him back.

"At least I smell manly, you just smell like an old jock strap." I grabbed my brother in a headlock and started giving him a noogie.

"Don't be an asshole, Bentley."

"I'm not. I'm just being your older brother," I said letting him go, "What do you want to do now?"

"Maggie's?"

"No, I was there for lunch." I tried to sound causal.

"Oh right, Whitney mentioned you went there for lunch. She also mentioned you were there with a pretty lady named Haley."

"Get that smug look off your face, Travis. We just had lunch after running some errands for the farm."

"Riiight," Travis snickered while hopping into the truck.

Driving my brother back to the farm, I decided to go check on the cows and see if the damn bull finally decided to make his way back to them. "When was the last time anyone checked to see if that bull went back with the herd?"

"I think the last time is when you did it. I was going to check when I got home."

I raised my eyebrow, "Want to go with me, we can take the four wheelers out?"

Haley

Bentley: I hate to do this, but I have to cancel our date today ☹

Haley: Why?

Bentley: Damn bull got out and we need to get him back in.

Haley: Have fun with that, lol.

Bentley: I'll make it up to you ☺

Haley: Bentley, it's fine really, I understand. We'll have our date the next chance we get, okay? ☺

Bentley: sorry ☹

Haley: lol no puppy eyes! I'll talk to you later.

Bentley: later.

It finally stopped raining on Friday, so after letting things dry on Saturday, I decided to tackle the sheds and scrape off all the old paint after church. I put my hair up in a ponytail, wore some old jean shorts that have seen better days with tons of holes in them, and a tank top. Then grabbed my flip-flops and sunglasses, making sure to fill up a water bottle.

Putting my headphones in and getting a good grip on the scraper, I threw on some tunes and away I went. I have no idea how much time passed, only that I was making some great headway. After drinking half of my water, I put on *Come and Get It* and went back to it while dancing and swinging my hips.

I started moving my hips more and more, letting the song take me over, and before I knew it, I had the scraper down, dancing and singing along with Selena Gomez. When the song finished, I pulled the ear buds out and drank the rest of the water. Turning around, I went to head into the house for more water.

"Ahhhhhhhhhhhhhhh!" I screamed dropping the water bottle and my ear buds. "Fuck, Bentley, you scared the living shit out of me." I placed my hands on my chest, trying to slow down my heartbeat.

"I didn't want to disturb the show I was getting. You looked beautiful being so carefree." Bentley smirked as he shoved his hands in his pockets. "Besides, I have a feeling you don't let go as often as you like, and I'd hate to take that away from you."

I looked over to Papa's dog, "Some guard dog you make," I grumbled.

"Well I may have bribed him with some beef jerky,"

Bentley said as he threw another piece at the dog.

"Figures," I mumbled.

After getting my breathing back to normal, I bent over and picked up the water bottle and ear buds. I heard Bentley clearing his throat. I turned around while covering my butt, "Bentley, were you checking me out?"

"Maybe."

"Well get the smirk off of your face, mister." I tried to sound like I had some authority in my voice.

"Nah, I liked the view," he teased back.

"So…" I said walking towards him, "What are you doing here?"

"Well I was hoping that I could take you out on a late lunch, then see if you were able to help me with something at my farm."

"You did, did you?" I answered, still slowly walking up to him.

"Mmm hmm," Bentley smiled, his eyes on my lips.

"Well, how about I offer you lunch, since I have leftovers and fresh lemonade I made yesterday," I answered back, looking at his lips while licking my bottom lip.

Bentley took hold of my hand with the ear buds in it then leaned in and kissed me. "I'd like that, Hales." I took his hand and we walked up to the house.

Opening the screen door for me Bentley asked, "What did you do yesterday?"

"Well, I did my laundry, tided up the house, made dinner; talked to my dad, my grandparents, and Carleigh."

"How is everyone doing?" he asked, taking a seat at the kitchen table.

"My dad is doing good, I think I'm going to visit him

for a bit when my grandparents get back. Grams said they are having a great time, but Papa is starting to get itchy to come home, and Carleigh…well, she's Carleigh."

"Who's Carleigh?"

I started washing my hands, "Carleigh is by best friend. We met freshman year of college; she's also a teacher, but she teaches at a public school in the city. I think she's coming to visit on Wednesday."

"I'd like to meet her."

"Well, be prepared, because she's one of a kind. You either love her, or hate her."

"Sounds like Curtis."

I grabbed two glasses from the cupboard and the lemonade from the fridge. I poured both glasses before returning to the fridge to grab out the leftovers.

"Haley, this looks good," Bentley complimented.

"It's nothing much. It's hard to cook just for yourself."

"Well, I love meatloaf, so anytime you're lonely, call me." Bentley chewed on his second meat loaf sandwich.

After drying the last dish, I asked Bentley, "What do you need help with today?"

"Well, after I dropped you off, my brother and I finally got this stupid bull back to the farm. Then he escaped again, which led to another shit day of catching him and me having to cancel our date. It wouldn't be a big deal if I didn't need his sperm."

"His sperm?" I ask confused.

"Yeah, we need to make sure he is still producing. We are getting a lot of open cows."

I leaned my hip on the counter, "I still don't understand, what do you need me for?"

"Really, I just need you to hold the cup in place."

"Ah, there is no one else that can help you?"

Bentley stepped in front of me and placed one hand on my hip, "You're not squeamish are you?"

"No."

"Then why do you suddenly look green?"

I cleared my throat, "Wouldn't you want Travis to help you, or maybe your dad?"

Bentley ran his other hand over my flushed cheek, "My brother had a date day planned with Whitney, and my parents went to a doctor's appointment. You're the only one that's available."

"Alright, let me go get some pants on." I turn to run upstairs, but not before Bentley's hand smacked my ass.

On the way to Bentley's farm, we talked more about our hobbies and interests.

"Let me get this straight, you learned how to crochet on YouTube?"

"Stop laughing, it's not that funny."

"Yes it is; crocheting is a grandma thing."

"It is not, take that back!" I punched him in the arm.

"Ouch," he whined while rubbing his arm.

"You might want to remember that, next time you tease me."

We pulled up to the farmhouse and I was barely able to get out of the truck before Bentley was at my side. "Bentley, this house is so charismatic. It's like something out of a book or a movie."

Bentley laughed, pulling me beside him, "Come on, beautiful girl. Let's get the bull out of the barn and do what we came here to do, then I'll give you a full tour."

I stopped, which made Bentley stop, "A full tour, and what all does that include, sir?"

Bentley smiled and kissed me, "Wouldn't you like to know?"

I kissed him back, "I sure would." We kissed a little more before Bentley pulled away and rested his forehead on mine.

"We better stop."

Opening the barn door I saw the biggest bull I've ever seen in my life, "Holy shit, Bentley, he's huge."

"He has the attitude to go with it, believe me." Bentley walked over to him with a handful of barley and offered it to the bull, "Don't you, big guy."

The bull let out a loud snort and moved one of his legs, which made me jump and scream a little. Bentley laughed at me once again, "He was just telling me he liked his treat. Don't be such a scaredy pants."

"I can't help it, he scares me."

Bentley walked over to me and put his arms around my waist, "I'll protect you."

"Promise?"

Putting one hand over his heart, "Promise."

I placed my hand over his and smiled.

We walked in front of the bull and Bentley put some barley in my hand. "Hold your hand flat and he will lick them off your hand."

I opened my hand flat and shakily reached out to the bull. I giggled when his tongue took a swipe of barley. "It feels funny."

"Have you never had a cow lick you before?" asked Bentley.

"When I was younger, we used to bottle feed the calves, but I don't remember it feeling like this. Usually, it's more wet and gross with saliva and the slimy milk replacer."

"I thought I saw cows on your grandparent's property?"

I kept watching the bull in amazement, "We do, but we only summer graze them, then Papa sells them in the fall." The bull finished the barley and I wiped my hand off on my pants.

"Are you okay here by yourself while I get a rope to pull him to the head gate?"

"Can I feed him more barley?"

"Sure." Bentley kissed my cheek, "Be right back."

I offered my hand again and the bull went back to licking the barley off it. I kept giggling as I slowly reached my other hand over the panel and tried to pet his head. The bull snorted really loud, louder than last time, and threw his head back. Which made me jump back and land on my butt.

Chapter Eight

Bentley

WATCHING HALEY INTERACT with the bull gave me such a warm sensation, and I couldn't help the smile on my face. Every time I turned around, this girl surprised me. Makes me wonder if I hadn't been such an asshole in high school if we would have dated, or at least been friends.

I led the bull into the cattle squeeze and made sure he was secure before I went back into the barn to get everything else I needed.

"Bentley, do you need any help?"

"No thanks, I think I got everything." I passed her a set of gloves, "You will want to put these on, though."

Taking them from my hands, she looked up and smiled. How is it this girl can take my breath away every time she smiles?

"Before we start I need to clip his preputial hair."

"Why?" Haley asked while bending over, looking at the bull.

"Because I need his semen in the cup and not tangled in the hair."

"In other words, you're man-scaping your bull?" she teased.

"Pretty much."

I was just putting the lube on the end of the probe when Haley looked at me,

"Is this safe, Bentley? I'm not going to lie, I'm scared to be sticking my hand in here."

I put everything down on the table and walked over to her, "Hales, I already promised you I would keep you safe."

"I know but…"

"With him in this device, he can't go anywhere, and he's not able to move his feet. There is no way he can hurt you. I would never put you in harm's way, sweetheart, ever."

"Okay."

"Haley, are his testicles getting tight?" I asked while turning on the probe.

"I-I don't know. I don't see any change."

I let out a snort, knowing I got her now; she's going to kill me. "Haley you can't see it, you need to actually feel them."

She looked at me glaring with an *are you kidding me* face. "What? I'm serious." I couldn't believe it; she's actually doing it.

"I think so," she said seriously.

"Okay that's good." God, it took all I could not to laugh out loud.

"Now, I need you to hold the cup under his penis. I'm

going to try to get him to come, but if this doesn't work then you may need to stroke him a little."

Haley jumped up and away from the bull, "No. No fucking way am I doing that, Bentley."

"I'm kidding, you don't have to do that...but you didn't need to feel his testicles, either."

"BENTLEY!"

Having her scream while hitting me was the funniest thing I have been a part of in a long time.

"Haley, that was the fucking funniest shit I ever saw, and here I thought Travis was gullible." I gasped out, bending over trying to catch my breath.

"I can't fucking believe you did that to me, Bentley. I'm so pissed off at you right now."

"Oh come on, I was joking. My dad did that to my mom once." Haley crossed her arms and huffed. "Okay, I'm sorry."

"Not funny," she growled.

"Should I tell you now that my mom didn't find it funny, either, when my dad did it to her, but it's one of my dad's favorite stories to tell us kids." That seemed to cool Haley down a little.

"Can we just finish this?" Haley stomped over back to the bull and grabbed the cup.

"Sure," I replied, still trying hard not to laugh.

"Asshole," she mumbled under her breath.

"NOW THAT I have what we need, I'm going to let him back in the corrals and then we can clean up and drop this off at the vet."

"Sure," Haley mumbled while taking off her gloves.

I wrapped my arm around her waist and dropped my head onto her shoulder, "You still mad at me?" I started kissing down her neck and nibbled on her collarbone.

"Yes."

I continued kissing and nibbling. She let out a soft moan as she tilted her head to the side, giving me better access. "How about now?"

"I'm still thinking."

I stepped out of her reach and walked over to let the bull out, "While you keep on thinking, I'm going to let the bull out." I looked back and smiled, and when I got one in return, I knew all was forgiven.

AFTER WE RETURNED from the vet, I gave Haley the full tour, stopping along the way to make out a little. Once the tour was over, I brought her into my room and lay her on my bed. I took off my t-shirt before I climbed on top of her.

I pushed her tank top up to kiss her belly, but she kept putting her hands in the way. "Bentley, please don't."

I kissed her fingers and slowly pried her hands away. "You're—*kiss*—beautiful—*kiss*—Haley. Every—*kiss*—inch—*kiss*—of—*kiss*—your body." I slid her tank top up even more before I tangled my fingers with hers and lifted her arms above her head.

I shifted Haley's hands so I was holding them with one hand, and pulled her tank top over her breasts with the other. I slipped one breast out of her bra before I sucked on her nipple. I could feel myself getting harder and harder as Haley wiggled underneath me. I let a moan out, knowing this was turning her on more and more.

She fought against my upper hand, trying to get her arms free. Letting go of her hands they went straight into my hair and brought me forward into a deep kiss. I ripped her tank top off of her before undoing her bra and letting her gorgeous tits free. I cupped both of them as she let out a moan.

Tweaking and sucking on her breasts made her moan louder as her hips moved involuntarily into my hard on, the sensations killing me with every thrust. Haley ran her hands down my back and ran her nails back up, sending shivers down my spine. "God, Hales, you feel so good," I whispered in her neck before kissing it some more.

I lifted up a little and moved my hands down to undo her jeans, so I could slide my hand into her pants, praying she was wearing a lacy thong.

"Bentley, stop."

I stopped my hands on the top of her jeans and started shifting myself off her. "I'm sorry …"

She cupped my face, cutting me off, "No, not that, someone's here." I lifted my head to hear what she was hearing.

"Travis, sometimes you are such an ass!" we could hear Whitney yell.

"I am not. That guy was totally flirting with you, and you let him," my brother reacted back.

"I was not, I was being nice."

"Whitney, don't be dumb. He was trying to pick you up right in front of me!"

I looked down at Haley as she tried to hide her face. I

pulled her hands away and kissed her.

"Are you calling me dumb, Travis?" Whitney fumed.

I groaned and put my head on Haley's chest. "I think I better go help. I don't see this going over well."

Haley let out a giggle. I put her breasts back into her bra and gave her my sad puppy look. She rolled her eyes and laughed.

I climbed off her, readjusted my jeans, mentally noting to kick my brother's ass for being responsible for leaving me like this. I leaned over Haley and passed her tank top to her before I tossed my shirt on myself as I opened my door.

"I'M NOT CALLING you dumb. I'm calling your actions dumb," argued my brother.

"I was giving him directions!" exclaimed Whitney.

"Whitney, we live in a town with four fucking streets. He doesn't need directions!"

I stepped into the living room and watched as Whitney took a step back and clammed up. "Sorry, Bentley, we didn't realize anyone was home."

Travis turned around and said, "Hey."

"Everything okay?" I asked, looking at Whitney.

"Yeah." breathed Whitney, "I'm just gonna go home."

Whitney grabbed her purse and opened the door.

"Stay," my brother called out. "Please."

"No. I think it's better if I go, I'll talk to you later. Good night, Bentley."

Hearing the door shut my brother let out a feral swear causing Haley to jump as she rounded the corner. "Shit, I'm sorry, Haley, I didn't see you there."

"You okay?" she asked.

"Yeah, I'm going for a walk. Catch you guys later." Travis pushed the door open and let the screen door slam behind him.

I walked up to Haley and brought her into my chest and kissed the top of her head. "I think you better take me home," she said.

I looked into her eyes, "Do I have to?"

"Yes. After your brother blows off some steam he's going to need someone to talk to."

"What if I'd rather talk to you?" I asked while grabbing her ass, pushing her body closer to my semi-hard erection.

Haley

"HE DID NOT?!" cried Carleigh.

"He did," I wailed while throwing the empty wine box at my best friend's head.

"God, I wish I could have seen your face when Bentley said you didn't need to feel the bull's testicles."

"Shut up!" I tried shouting, but couldn't because we were both on the floor, laughing hard.

THE NEXT MORNING, I could barely lift my head off of the pillow, "Someone shoot me," I groaned, rolling back over.

"Come on, sleepy head. I brought you some coffee."

I slowly sat up, grabbing the cup, smelling the aroma. "Why aren't you shit for wear, too?"

"Because I'm not a light weight like you," Carleigh slapped my leg, "come on get up, you can drink your coffee on the porch with me while I watch all those football players paint."

"You know they are all under age, right?" I asked as I put on my slippers.

"I know, doesn't mean I can't watch them flex their muscles." She laughed as she headed down the stairs.

"That is why you can't teach high school!" I yelled at her.

Pulling my hair into a messy bun then brushing my teeth and washing my face, I headed downstairs.

"Good morning," Carleigh chimed as she poured me another cup of coffee.

I looked at her and growled. We both turned when we heard the screen door open.

"Haley, I have the boys finishing up..." Bentley stood in the kitchen just looking at me. "What happened to you?"

Carleigh cheerfully stepped in front of Bentley and introduced herself. "I'm Carleigh. Hangover-head's best friend."

He stuck out his hand, "I'm..."

"Coach Knight. Yes, I have heard lots about you."

Bentley looked over at me and lifted his eyebrow.

"Check the ego, Bentley, want some coffee?" I offered before weaving into a kitchen chair and putting my head on the table.

"Ouch, what has your panties in such a twist?" ribbed Bentley.

"Oh nothing, this is just what happens when you mix a box of wine, four shots of vodka, and one courageous shot of Grams' moonshine," laughed Carleigh.

I could do nothing but moan some more.

Bentley walked over and started rubbing my shoulders, "Is there anything I can do?"

I just moved my head back and forth, "No."

Carleigh brought me over a glass of orange juice and a few Advil. I lifted my head and took them, "Thanks."

"What's the plan today?" asked Carleigh.

I groaned again.

"Don't you groan at me, young lady, I only have today to chill with you before I head back tomorrow."

I stood up from the kitchen table, "I'm going to go shower." I announced.

"What some help…scrubbing your back?" Bentley offered.

"I think I got it," I said climbing the stairs.

AFTER USING UP all the hot water, I was finally starting to feel human again. Brushing my teeth for the second time, I braided my hair before heading back downstairs. I rounded the corner to the kitchen when I heard Bentley and Carleigh talking outside on the porch.

"Bentley, I'm serious, she's my best friend. I will not let you hurt her."

"I won't."

"I don't think you understand…"

Bentley cut her off, *"I get it, I was an asshole. I'm not that person anymore."*

"Really?" I could hear the sarcasm in Carleigh's voice.

"I'm not. I would never intentionally hurt her."

"I guess time will tell, but be warned if you hurt her, I will not hesitate to drive down here and break your face. Are we clear, Bentley?"

I walked onto the porch before Bentley had time to respond, "Hey, what are you guys talking about?"

"I was just telling Bentley how I plan to come back to visit, before we go back to school."

I smiled as I sat in between them on the porch swing. "Great, then we can hit up the blueberry festival with Grams when you come back."

Bentley put his coffee cup on the floor and stood, "Thanks for the coffee, but I better go and check on the boys. They should be done painting by the end of the day."

"Wow, I can't believe how much those boys can get done. It feels like every time I give them a job, I need to have another one ready."

Carleigh laughed, "Well, hon, you have like fifteen of them."

"I guess."

"What do you want us to do with the leftover paint?" asked Bentley.

"You can put it in the shop for now. Papa can move it where he wants when he comes back."

"Carleigh, it was nice to meet you." Bentley shook her hand.

"Like wise. I hope to see you again, maybe when I

come back out?" she suggested.

"Sure, maybe we can all go for drinks, or something."

I got up and walked over to Bentley before he hit the last step. "Bentley?"

He turned around, "Yeah?"

"Is everything okay? I mean, I know that sometimes Carleigh can come off as..."

He cupped my face, "Everything is fine, baby. I'll catch you later?"

"Okay." I watched him walk away before I turned to my best friend.

"What was that?" I demanded.

"What was what?"

"Don't be coy with me, Ms. Carleigh-May. I heard you two talking while I was in the kitchen." I threatened.

"Hasn't Grams ever told you it's rude to eavesdrop?"

"Carleigh…"

"Don't use your teacher voice on me."

I leaned against the rail, my arms folded across my chest, waiting for her to answer the question.

"Fine," she puffed, "I was just explaining the reservations I have about Bentley."

"That's not your place."

"Really? Because after watching you for the past six years, I beg to differ. You have never let anyone close to you, and by that, I mean a man."

"I'm not a virgin," I seethed.

"You may as well be. Have you ever been in love? Like true love where you feel comfortable running around naked, or texting dirty pictures?"

"What does that have to do with anything?" I voiced.

"Everything." Carleigh got up and threw her arms around me. "Bentley was a bully, a jackass, or whatever you want to call him. Can't you see he left you with some damage."

"I am not damaged," I almost yelled at her.

"You are," she answered quietly, "Anyone that is, or has been, bullied will always walk away with some sort of damage, and yours is your body issues."

"I don't have body issues."

"Is that so?" she argued.

"Yes!"

"Fine, then take off your top right now."

"I'm not taking my top off."

"That's what I thought." Carleigh grabbed her coffee cup and Bentley's and went inside.

CARLEIGH AND I spent the rest of the afternoon at the farmer's market and picked up a few knickknacks before she left. I helped her with her bags and put them in the back seat of her car.

"I'm sorry about earlier," she said.

"I understand. You are only looking out for me," I said, shutting the car door.

"I was, but I still shouldn't have said those things," Carleigh looked down to the ground, "and I don't think you're damaged."

I brought her into a hug, "I know, and I love you."

"Forgive me?"

"There is nothing to forgive. You are my sister, a *much* older sister that just annoys me, but loves me to death."

"That I do."

"Call me when you get home?"

"I will."

I watched as she pulled out of the yard and headed back to the city.

Chapter Nine

Bentley

I'M GLAD IT'S Friday, it was a long week with the boys. They lost focus by Wednesday and were ready to blow off some steam. I had to keep reminding them why we were at Wells' ranch. I'm so glad Coach Dudley is going to take over starting Monday.

Haley and I haven't really had a chance to talk since Wednesday. I was hoping to get some alone time with her after her friend left, but something always managed to come up. I'm hoping to tonight, though, before her grandparents come home on Tuesday.

I was sitting on Curtis' couch, fiddling with my phone debating if I should text her, or just go see her. I chose to text and see if she'd flirt back.

Bentley: Hey pretty lady.
Haley: Hi :)
Bentley: What are you doing?

Haley: Just heading into the shower.
Bentley: What are you wearing?
Haley: Seriously?
Bentley: Yeah:)
Haley: Well I'm heading into the shower, so I'm naked.
Bentley: Want company!?!!
Haley: To what …wash my back?
Bentley: I'll wash more than that if you want.
Haley: I'm good.
Bentley: You sure? I can be there real quick.
Haley: I'm sure you can ;)
Bentley: Please…
Haley: I'll text you when I'm done :)
Bentley: Wanna hang out tonight?
Haley: I'll see, after my shower.
Bentley: You're killing me here.
Haley: I'm sure you'll survive. Text in a bit.

It must have been over an hour since she last texted. What could possibly take so long? I ate, showered and *took the dog out for a walk,* if you know what I mean.

Bentley: Are you drowning yet?
Bentley: I'm getting worried…
Haley: *picture sending*

My mouth hung open as she sent me a picture of her in the tub with her legs sticking out and, of course, the bubbles had to cover other things. I was not expecting this at all. Haley has a naughty side. I bet it has to do with all those books she reads.

Bentley: Nice!
Haley: Just decided on a bath instead, feels good.
Bentley: I bet it's real lonely in there…
Haley: No, I have Adam to keep me company.
Bentley: Adam?
Haley: Um-hmm

I sat there for a few minutes trying to remember who the hell Adam was, then I remembered last week when I brought Haley breakfast, she was reading that romance book.

Bentley: Are you finished reading yet?
Haley: I think so; my bath water is starting to get chilly.
Bentley: I can come warm you up :)
Haley: I was actually thinking of having a campfire.
Bentley: Even better, I'll bring a blanket.
Haley: Sounds good, give me an hour?
Bentley: I already did.
Haley: Funny, smart guy.
Bentley: See you soon :)

I got up put some jeans on, my old Longhorns sweatshirt, and my ball cap. I didn't want to ruin the chance of Haley wanting to run her fingers through my hair with goop in it. On my way out the door, I called my mom.
"Hello?"
"Hi, Mom."

"How are you, sweetie?"

"I'm good. The reason why I'm calling is I was wondering if you could make me your hot chocolate, please?"

"Sure. I haven't made that for you boys since you were kids." I could hear the smile in my mom's voice.

"I'm going over to see Haley and spend some time with her before her grandparents get back on Tuesday."

"Ohhh," my mom teased.

"It's not like that," I assured her, because my mom doesn't need to know what my actual plans are, even though she probably does. "We are just going to light a campfire and maybe roast a few marshmallows."

"It's nine o'clock, a little late to just be dropping by, son."

"Is it?" I played dumb, "I didn't realize. Good thing fires are best at night."

"You know, when your father was younger, he use to come over when it was late, just to have hot chocolate."

"Mom." I eww'ed at her.

"What? It's the truth."

"But I don't need to hear about it." I felt a shiver go down my body.

"Oh, Bentley," she giggled.

"I'll see you in a few, Mom. Do you need anything from town?"

"No, Dad and I are going back to the city tomorrow."

"Is everything okay?"

"Oh yes, he is taking me out on a *hot chocolate* date."

"Mom!"

I could hear her laughing before she hung up the phone.

On my way out to the farm I got to thinking that maybe my parents leaving the farm wasn't such a bad thing for them. Ever since my mom finally made a decision, the tone in her voice is happier, she has a small bounce back in her step, and I don't remember the last time my dad took her out on a date.

When I pulled into our driveway, I saw the barn light was on so I drove over there to turn it off. I hopped out of the truck and saw my dad sitting in there with the radio on.

"Hey, Dad." I walked over and sat beside him on a square bale.

"Son."

"What are you doing out here?"

"Just thinking."

"About what?" I asked, leaning over picking up a piece of straw to fiddle with.

"On life, and where it can lead you."

"A little young to be thinking about something this heavy, aren't you?"

My dad placed his hand on my knee and tapped it a few times, "You are never too young, or too old, to decide what you want out of life, son. Every day is a new day, to have a fresh beginning; it's just up to us if we want it."

My dad and I sat there just listening to an old George Strait song on the radio.

"You know, son, I never thought I'd have to say goodbye to this farm. I thought I'd work it 'til the day I died. Every treasured memory I have of you, Travis, and of your mom is all here, Bentley. You have no idea what it feels like to pack it in."

I sat quietly, trying to take in what my dad was saying.

"Dad you may not be able to work on the farm anymore, but your memories will always be there for you."

"But I never thought I wouldn't be able to work on it beside you. Teach Travis the things I should be teaching him, and running around after my grandchildren on the front lawn."

"Dad, you can still do those things."

"Can I?" my dad said with his head down, looking at his boots. "You have no idea how frustrating it is to see things fall through your fingers."

"I think I do, Dad," I quietly whispered, while looking at him.

"I know, son. I can't be more grateful to you for turning down your dream and coming home."

"You make it sound like a sacrifice."

"Well, wasn't it?"

I got up and paced the floors, "Of course not, Dad. I would do anything for you and Mom, even if the meant giving up my career."

"But you're not happy, Bentley. I can see that."

"I'm starting to be." I breathed out.

"Look, I know I've been a hard ass; hell, Travis hardly looks at me anymore. Your mother and I are drifting apart…I have so much to apologize for."

"Dad, we're family, we'll always forgive you."

Dad walked up to me and engulfed me in a hug, "I'm so sorry, Bentley."

"I love you, Dad."

"I love you, Son." We parted as my dad pushed away the tears on his face.

"How do I get Travis to forgive me?"

"Start by talking to him, Dad. I've learned a lot about myself these past two weeks. I've seen my good and the bad has been brought to my attention, and the best thing I learned is always be honest, and you can't get others to forgive you until you forgive yourself."

"Does this have to do with a pretty blonde I hear your mom and Maggie talking about?"

"Maybe, Dad, just maybe."

"I'd glad, son. It's nice to have someone that can keep you grounded."

"Do you have a plan for you and Mom?"

"Yes, tomorrow I'm taking her shopping then treating her to a spa day. Afterwards, we'll catch dinner and a movie. I also booked us at one of those bed and breakfast things that she's always looking at."

"Good for you, Dad."

"Thanks, son. Your mom more than deserves it."

"You deserve just as much as she does."

Dad grabbed me around the shoulders as we walked out of the barn. "Let's shut things down, and I'll walk to the house with you."

Haley

IT'S BEEN OVER an hour and Bentley still isn't here yet. I wonder what is keeping him. I went outside to the fire pit and started making a fire. After I got that going, I grabbed a couple chairs and went back into the house for the things I needed to make s'mores.

I was on my second s'more when I finally saw truck lights coming up the driveway as Buddy barked. "Now you bark, you silly boy. You haven't barked the whole time we've had company these past two weeks." I put down the sticky goodness and pet the dog on the head, "Some guard dog you make, Buddy."

I heard Bentley open his truck door and shut it before he made his way to the fire. With the glow of the fire, I could see his outline as he moved closer. He stopped in front of me and licked my bottom lip. "You had some marshmallow there."

I wiped my lip, "Thanks."

He set a thermos on the table along with a big bulky blanket and a bag. "I thought maybe you backed out," I said.

Bentley grabbed my s'more and took a bite, "Sorry I'm late. I had a talk with my dad."

"Is everything okay?"

"It will be," he smiled.

I walked over to him and kissed him. Grabbing me by the waist he brought me in closer. "What did you bring?" I asked, looking over his shoulder.

"My mom's hot chocolate, you'll love it."

"And what's in the bag?"

"I figured you'd be making s'mores, so I grabbed some of her homemade chocolate chip cookies. We can use them instead of the graham crackers."

"I've never made them with cookies before."

Bentley kissed me again, "You'll love them."

He slapped my butt, "How about you go grab us some

mugs and I'll make you another s'more with mom's cookies."

"Okay," I giggled excitedly, before running into the house hearing him laugh behind me.

By the time I came out, Bentley had the blanket all spread out, candles flickering on the table and he was waiting for me with his hand reaching out for me.

"What's all this?" I asked.

"Our first official date."

Leading me over to the blanket, Bentley poured us both some hot chocolate before snuggling in behind me.

"Your hot chocolate," he whispered into my neck.

"Thank you."

Tucking his arms around me, I held my mug closer as we watch the flames dance.

"This is the same blanket my parents used on their first date."

"Really?" I asked.

"Mom said to bring it, it brought her good luck."

"So far I think it's doing a good job," I said looking into Bentley's eyes.

"Me, too."

We sat and talked about everything and anything. We talked about his football days in Texas, and what I really wanted out of my teaching career. Bentley expressed how he felt about his family farm, and what it would mean if he stayed, or if he went. I told him how I wanted to stay here and eventually take over for my grandparents as I raised my own family one day.

"You know, Hales, I don't think I've ever been this honest with someone besides Travis. It feels good to share these things with you." He spoke into my hair as he played with it.

"I feel the same, Bentley. I have a hard time letting people in. I'd rather sit quietly in a corner and watch than be part of the crowd. But with you, I feel my thoughts are safe."

Bentley turns me around to face him. I stared into his eyes, watching the flames flicker in them, "Bentley, I think I'm falling for you." He cupped my head and kissed me. He started out slow, asking permission to enter my mouth. I granted it by sucking on his tongue.

He laid us down on the blanket and hovered over me. Fanning out my hair with his fingers, he whispered, "You're beautiful." My fingers ached to touch him, I grabbed the bottom of his sweatshirt and started pulling it up. I only got halfway before Bentley sat up and took it off completely, along with his t-shirt.

I ran my fingers over his chest before moving down and counting each stomach muscle. "I love when you touch me, Hales." I sat up and laid kisses on his chest as he rubbed my back slowly as he pulled my sweater off. "You're not wearing a bra," he mumbled into my hair.

"I know." I replied kissing his chest.

Sitting up on my knees, I undid his jeans before sliding my hands in, grabbing his ass cheeks and giving them a tight squeeze, making Bentley growl. I slowly moved my hand to the front and grabbed his hard penis, stroking it a few times. "Haley, you need to stop." I withdrew my hand and slid down his zipper and pushed his jeans to his knees before I dropped my mouth to his cock.

Bentley leaned over me, pushing down my sweat

pants, gliding his fingers around my body until they found my clit and slowly started making circles. Moaning around his cock, Bentley picked me up and placed me on the table pulling my sweats off the rest of the way before kicking his jeans over to the pile on the grass.

Carrying me over to the blanket Bentley kissed me, starting at my neck moving down my arm, over my chest and down my stomach as we lay down together. I ran my fingers through his hair, arching my back with every kiss, every gentle touch. "Bentley," I breathed.

"God, Hales you take my breath away," he said, kissing his way back up. "Never have I ever felt this connection with anyone."

I placed my hands around his neck bringing his lips over to mine, "Make love to me, Bentley." Slowly he entered me and my breathing hitched. Bentley stopped and looked me in the eyes. "Keep going…give this to me, Bentley, please."

Thrusting slowly, Bentley moved and captured every emotion I was feeling. "I'll give you anything you ask, sweetheart."

LYING ON HIS chest, I watched the fire die, listening to our heart beats slowly returning to normal. Bentley moved my hair from my face, "That was…"

"Don't say anything, let's just lay here and enjoy the moment."

He kissed the top of my head and pulled the blanket around us as I drifted off to sleep.

Chapter Ten
Bentley

WAKING UP, I felt Haley breathing lightly on top of me, knowing she was still asleep I watched as the sun rose, welcoming a new day. I slowly twirled her hair around my fingers watching the glow of the remaining embers of the fire.

I thought about what my past held, and what my future offered. I thought about what my dad said, and how my mom always gave me her support and that Travis was leaving next fall.

I asked myself, how would my parents be able to afford to put Travis through school if I left the farm? Where would my dad find peace? Where would my mom play with her grandchildren? All these thoughts were coming faster and faster.

I couldn't breathe; I had to get out of here. I tried slowly moving away from Haley, but she whimpered and moved in deeper. I was starting to panic, my breathing picked up. I tried calming myself down, but I couldn't. I needed to get up. I needed to breathe.

Taking Haley, I moved her off me, careful not to wake her so I could leave without her questioning me. I know it's a total douche move, but I didn't want to see the pain in her eyes when she realized I was leaving.

Opening her eyes she lit up with the biggest smile when I came into focus. "Morning," she moved in to kiss me, but I pulled back. "Bentley?"

"I need to go. I'm sorry, Haley." I got up and put on my pants on.

Haley covered herself with the blanket and stood looking at me, "Why? What did I do wrong?" I could hear the tremor in her voice. I turned around and lifted the one tear that fell from her cheek before I turned and walked away.

"Run, run like you always do, Bentley!" she yelled at me, her voice full of emotion.

"I'm not running," I answered her.

"Bull shit!"

I turned around and faced her, "What is that supposed to mean?"

She calmly walked over to me, "Bentley, you are a good man, you came home when your family needed you, no questions asked, but now, instead of making a decision, you run."

"I stayed," I argued.

"Really? Because instead of figuring out what you want, you stayed away and lived with Curtis these past two weeks."

"I'm figuring out what *I want!*"

Haley took a step back as if I just slapped her in the

face, "I-I thought when you came here last night you made your decision," she choked out.

Stepping back I opened my truck door and heard Haley pleading, "Make a decision, Bentley. Pick something, just make a choice." I kept my head down to the ground. "Pick me…take a chance on us."

I got into my truck without looking back and left Haley standing there in my mother's *good luck* blanket.

Epilogue

Haley

IT'S BEEN THREE weeks since Bentley left, and I haven't heard from him. The football team has finished up their commitments with Papa and the ranch looks great. I didn't help much after Papa came back, it was too hard to see Travis and not ask him if he'd heard from Bentley, and if he's okay.

Reaching into my closet, I grabbed Mrs. Knight's blanket and hugged it one last time. It was time I let Bentley go, and of all the pain he's caused. Walking into the kitchen I let Grams know I was heading to town and I would be back later.

Walking into the diner, it felt like I was saying goodbye. I could feel tears building up, but I managed to keep them at bay. "Hey, Haley." Whitney waved.

"Hi, is Maggie here?"

"Yeah she is in the back, in her office."

"Would it be okay if I went to go see her?"

"Girl, we all know how much she loves you, of course

it's alright. Want me to bring you anything?"

"No, it's okay. I'm just returning something." I lifted the blanket in my arms.

"Okay, see you later then." she waved off.

"Thanks." I walked back to Maggie's office with my head hanging low.

I knocked on the door before slowly opening it. I saw another woman around Maggie's age sitting on the couch beside her drinking coffee. "I'm sorry, I didn't mean to interrupt. I just want to drop off this blanket for..."

"Bentley's mom." the lady offered.

"Umm yes. How did you know?" I asked placing the blanket on Maggie's desk.

The lady stood and walked over to me, "Sweetheart, I'm Bentley's mom."

The tears started running down my face. I wiped them away as quickly as I could, "I'm sorry I should have returned it weeks ago."

"I understand why you didn't." she brought me into a hug when I broke down and cried into her arms.

"I'm just going to leave you two alone. Take as much time as you need." Maggie offered before quietly shutting the door.

After blowing my nose, I looked to Bentley's mom, "I didn't mean to cry like that, I've been crying more than usual lately." I stuttered, "My name is Haley Wells."

"Hello." she smiled, "My name is Charlotte, and my husband's name is Will. I'm assuming you know our other son, Travis."

"Yes, ma'am, he's a great kid. You should be proud of both your boys."

"We are, very much so."

Things were quiet for a moment, "I should…"

"Why don't we sit and talk?" asked Charlotte.

Together we walked over to the couch. "May I offer you some coffee?" she asked.

"Please."

"I hear that you are a teacher."

"I am, I've been teaching in the city for the last few years."

"Do you enjoy it?" she asked pouring coffee into a mug.

"Very much."

"When do you go back?"

"I'm not sure." I answered before taking the mug from her.

"What makes you say that?"

I looked up at her, "Mrs. Harris offered me a position at the elementary school, last week."

"That's great, Haley."

"I told her that I would need to think about it.

"Have you given it any thought?" I shifted away from her a little, feeling a little uncomfortable having such a conversation with Bentley's mom.

"I didn't mean to be rude." Charlotte spoke.

"I…I don't know what to do." I muttered.

"Why not?"

"I'd really like to stay here. I love it here, but…"

"Why don't you stay then?" I looked down at the floor. "Is it because of Bentley?"

I continued to look at the floor, "I don't want to be the reason why he doesn't come back home." I whispered.

Charlotte gasped, "Is that what you think, that Bentley left because of you?"

I wiped more tears that ran down my face, before I looked up at her.

"Oh dear, you fell in love with him." I nodded my head.

Charlotte brought me into her arms, "Honey, I promise you, you are not the reason why he left. If anything, he'll come back for you."

"I'm not so sure I believe that."

Bentley's mom tipped my head so she could look at me in the eyes. "Haley, he was starting to fall in love with you."

"How do you know?"

"Because, Will and I have seen many changes in our son. Ever since he met you he smiles more, laughs more with his brother, and he started remembering the good life on the farm, instead of all the bad."

"But we've only really known each other for two weeks."

"Sometimes that's all it takes. Has he told you about Will and what we offered to him?"

"Yes."

"Hon, that's the reason why he left. Not because of you. He fears he will take things away from Travis, Will, and myself if he decides he wants out. But what he doesn't realize, Haley, is that we are all okay with saying goodbye to the farm."

"But I thought…"

"I know what you thought sweetheart, that's why it's taken so long to return the blanket."

I smiled at her.

"We only want what is best for our son, and we think it's you and the farm. But we can't make that decision for him this time, like we did when Will first was hurt. He needs to decide this on his own. He needs to come back on his own terms."

"I'm not sure I can wait, and then just have him walk away again."

"I would never ask that of you, Haley, or anyone else. You need to do what's good for you, and if you think staying here and teaching is where you want to be, then, Haley, stay here. Don't give away your happiness over a stupid boy, even if it is my son."

I giggled, "Thank you."

Maggie opened the door, "Is everything going okay in here?"

"All is good, Maggie." Charlotte reassured while smiling at me.

"You know, Bentley never did tell me how you two know each other."

Maggie sat on the other side of me. "Charlotte and I have been best friends since we were toddlers."

"Oh."

"I bet you are wondering why you and Charlotte have ever met before, or why you and Bentley didn't know each other as kids?" asked Maggie.

"Yeah."

"That's kind of my fault," replied Maggie.

"How so?" I asked.

"Your dad came home to visit after college and brought your mom, Jennifer, home to meet everyone. Jennifer and I got into a fight and your dad was put in the middle."

"What happened?"

"I thought she wasn't good enough for your dad, and I let my emotions get the best of me and I punched her."

"No way, Maggie, you would never hit anyone." I argued.

"Well, I did that day."

"She has a good right hook, if I say so myself." Charlotte said.

"Anyways, Jennifer said it was either her or me, and your dad…"

"Chose her." I whispered, "A lot of good that did."

"After that visit, your dad hardly ever came back home. When she left…I guess it was easier to stay away."

I placed my hand on Maggie's, "Do you miss him, my dad?"

"Every day."

A New Chapter

Haley

AFTER VISITING MY dad for a few days I decided Charlotte was right and I took the job Mrs. Harris offered. I will now be the new second grade teacher at Myers Elementary School. I also applied for, and got, the track coach position at the high school. Both will start in three weeks, and I couldn't be more excited. Life is finally feeling like it's in place, except for one little thing. The pregnancy test that's in my hand, reading I was going to have a baby.

"Haley, I loaded the last box in the truck." Travis said through the bathroom door.

"Thanks, Travis, I'll be right out."

I tucked the stick into my purse and looked in the mirror with a huge smile. I am going to be a mom.

I did the last check around my apartment before locking the door on my past for the last time. "I'm going to miss you," cried Carleigh as we held hands down the stairs.

"You can always come teach with me at Myers."

"No thanks. I love visiting there, but no way will I ever be a small town girl."

"I love you." I brought Carleigh in for a hug, "Thank you for everything."

AFTER CURTIS PROPOSED to Loran, he moved in with her, leaving his house vacant. With the help of Charlotte he agreed to rent it out to me, after he paid for a thorough cleaning and a new paint job.

After the last box was put away, I flopped on the couch.

"Tired?" asked Charlotte.

"Yeah, who knew moving could be this exhausting."

"I don't know why you're so tired, it's not like you moved anything heavy." complained Travis coming out from the kitchen with Cullen.

"Shut up." Whitney said behind him, slapping him on the back of the head.

Charlotte, Will, and I just laughed.

The front door opened and my grandparents walked in, "Hi, Sweetie, we just thought we'd bring you over some groceries."

"You guys didn't need to do that." I said getting up, hugging them both.

"Don't be silly, child, of course we did." Papa huffed before hugging me.

"Welcome home Haley." Grams smiled.

THE NIGHT BEFORE my first day of work, Charlotte, Maggie, and Whitney stopped in and we all had dinner together. Drying the last dish I asked Charlotte, "Is it weird that we're friends?"

"Why would you ask me that?"

"I just mean with Bentley not talking to me, and him not returning home yet. Is it weird that I'm friends with you guys? I feel close to you all, and I'd hate to be stepping on Bentley's toes or something."

Rinsing out the last of the sink Charlotte replied, "You are not stepping on Bentley's toes. We asked you to be a part of our lives, if it pisses Bentley off, too bad for him. He cannot tell his mother who to be friends, or not to be friends with."

"Okay." I said quietly.

Charlotte gave me a hug, "You are very special to us, Haley. We love you as much as we love Whitney."

"But I'm not with..."

"Doesn't matter, sweetheart."

Whitney and Maggie came walking into the kitchen with empty drinking glasses. "Haley what do you have planned with the spare room? I was thinking that maybe when I'm done school, I can move in with you." asked Whitney.

"I'm...umm" I looked over to Maggie then Whitney before Charlotte, "I'm going to be making it into a nursery."

The kitchen was dead silent. The only noise I heard

was the beating of my own heart against my chest.

"Haley?" asked Charlotte, "Did I hear you right?"

"Yes." I whispered, "I'm sorry, I know Bentley should find out first."

Charlotte took a step back and grabbed her purse off the counter digging out her cell phone, dialing someone. "Will. You tell that son of ours to get his ass home!" She hung up as fast as she'd dialed. I stood and watched her, panicking inside.

"Don't look at me like that, child, I'm going to be a grandma, and I couldn't be happier."

"Really?" I asked, shocked, "I didn't plan this, to trap him or anything…" I rattled on.

"Why in the world would you think that? I know you would never do something like that. Haley you don't have an evil thought in that pretty head of yours."

"But I don't want anyone thinking…"

"No one will think that, and I'll make sure of it." Maggie said while looking over to Whitney. "Anything else we should celebrate?"

Whitney put her hands up, "No babies here."

"Just checking," Maggie laughed.

"Oh Lord." Charlotte laughed.

I'VE BEEN TEACHING now for a little over a month, which leaves me eleven and a half weeks pregnant. I've been training the track team a little harder this past week because we have a meet coming up, and every practice this week has run fifteen minutes longer than normal.

I've heard Bentley has come back home and decided to stay and take over the farm, but also decided it needed to be downsized to make it more feasible. I have yet to hear from him, or see him. I've tried really hard to stay hidden at the track this past month while football practice has been going on, so I don't have to risk running into Bentley until I'm ready.

I'm glad that Charlotte and her family understand, and are willing to visit me at home instead of me going to theirs. "Are you going to keep hiding?" asked Travis grabbing a water bottle off the ground.

"No, and what are you talking about?" I lied.

"Well it's hot as shit out here, and you are wearing a t-shirt over your tank top, plus that ridiculous ball cap." Travis laughed while flipping the ball cap off my head.

"I just like to wear two shirts."

"Haley, no one likes to wear two shirts on days like today. Hell, I even hate wearing my football gear on days like today."

I leaned closer to him, "I don't want anyone to notice. I'm not ready yet."

"No one will notice, you hardly even have a bump. The only reason we see it is because we see you almost every day."

"I just…"

"I know you don't want Bentley finding out until he can get his head out of his ass, but it's not worth overheating over it."

"I'm not overheating." I said lifting my armpits to see if they have sweat stains.

"You're face says different. Are you drinking enough water?"

I lifted my empty water bottle, "Yes, Uncle Travis."

"Good, just take the t-shirt off, Haley, no one will notice and if they do, we'll just say it's all those cheeseburgers and strawberry milkshakes you inhale."

"I do not." I grumbled.

"Do to."

"You sure?" I asked, nervous.

"Positive."

I looked around before taking off the t-shirt and leaving on the tank top. It felt great to feel the breeze on my bare arms.

"Doesn't that feel better?" asked Travis.

"Yes."

"See I told you…"

"Why is half of my football team still over here, instead of at practice like they should be?" Bentley yelled as he stomped over.

Travis and I spun around, "Shit." I said to Travis under my tongue.

"I don't think he knows you are the new track coach." Travis leaned over and laughed.

Find out what happens next in

Part Two

Thank You!

I'D LIKE TO keep this short and sweet because this book is really for Lacy.

First I'd like to thank fellow author Lynda LeeAnne for allowing me to use her words from Adam, Enough Said, which is one of Lacy's favorite books and her favorite sex scene. Ha-ha I got you again, Lacy.

Robin from Wicked by Design & Raelene from word·play by 77peaches for torturing me in decision-making, and Natalie of Island Lovelies Book Club. You ladies have been absolutely wonderful to work with, and I'm so looking forward to working with you again. My beta readers once again you guys make me laugh with your comments. My readers, followers and bloggers thank you for everything. Words cannot express the love that I have for each and every one of you.

My dear sweet children and husband, you are I'm sure the most patient family a mom/wife can ever ask for. I appreciate everything that you offer up, to make me smile when I am about to pull my hair out. I love you ...In fact, I love you *most*!

HOW TO FIND SHAWNTE

www.facebook.com/shawnteborrisauthor

shawnteborrisauthor.com

author.shawnteborris@gmail.com

SOME FAVORITE BOOKS OF LACY'S

LYNDA LEEANNE:
Lexi, Baby
Trish, Just Trish
Adam, Enough Said

R.L MATHEWSON:
NFH (series): Playing for Keeps
Perfection
Checkmate
Truce
PYTE/SENTINAL(series): Tall, Dark & Lonley
Without Regret
Tall Dark & Heartless
EMS: Sudden Response
HollyWood Hearts (series): A Humble Heart
A Reclusive Heart

ELIZABETH JAMES:
Love by Design
Life by Design
Forever by Design
Secrets of a Hart
Chasing Rain-TBA

JEANENÉ MAINVILLE:
All For You

ALEXIS ALEXANDER:
Strong Enough
Stronger – TBA

LISA HARLEY:
Destined to Change
Destined to Succeed
Real Men Wear Pink
Four Letters

JL MONRO:
The Perfection of Love

LAUREL ULEN CURTIS:
The One Place
The One Girl
Impossible
A is for Alpha Male

SARAH GOODMAN:
Life's Perfect Plan
Life's Next Chapter

KELLY ELLIOTT:
Wanted
Saved
Faithful
Cherished

Made in the USA
Charleston, SC
09 May 2014